I AM PRIN

CHERIE PRIEST ILLUSTRATED BY KALI CIESEMIER

 ARTHUR A. LEVINE BOOKS AN IMPRINT OF SCHOLASTIC INC.

FOR LUKE AND CLAUDIA.
JUST BECAUSE.

CONTENTS

CHAPTER ONE
....1

CHAPTER TWO
....15

CHAPTER THREE
....20

CHAPTER FOUR
....36

CHAPTER FIVE
....50

CHAPTER SIX
....53

CHAPTER SEVEN
....56

CHAPTER EIGHT
....61

CHAPTER NINE
....70

CHAPTER TEN
....77

CHAPTER ELEVEN
....98

CHAPTER TWELVE
....110

CHAPTER THIRTEEN
....124

CHAPTER FOURTEEN
....126

CHAPTER FIFTEEN
....133

CHAPTER SIXTEEN
....142

CHAPTER SEVENTEEN
....144

CHAPTER EIGHTEEN
....156

CHAPTER NINETEEN
....166

CHAPTER TWENTY
....173

CHAPTER TWENTY-ONE
....179

CHAPTER TWENTY-TWO
....186

CHAPTER TWENTY-THREE
....198

CHAPTER TWENTY-FOUR
....206

CHAPTER TWENTY-FIVE
....223

ONE

Libby Deaton and May Harper invented Princess X in fifth grade, when Libby's leg was in a cast, and May had a doctor's note saying she couldn't run around the track anymore because her asthma would totally kill her.

Their PE teacher sent them into exile on the little-kids playground — where the kindergarten teacher sat in the shade, reading a romance novel with a mostly naked man on the cover. A crowd of nervous six-year-olds watched the newcomers from behind the swing set, big-eyed, silent, and ready to bolt. For all the little kids knew, fifth graders were capable of anything.

But Libby and May just sat off to the side, against the brick wall, their legs stretched out across the asphalt. They had nothing to do. Nowhere to go. No one to talk to but each other, and it wasn't like they were friends or anything. Libby had changed schools after her parents bought a new house, and May had just moved to Seattle from Atlanta. They barely knew each other's names.

Still, there was solidarity in boredom, and sidewalk chalk lay all over the four-square court that no one was using right that minute. May kicked a piece that some tiny Picasso had ditched, and then crushed it with the heel of her shoe. The cement turned a satisfying cherry red, like the pavement was bleeding. She leaned her leg toward a blue piece, ready to smash it into dust as well — but Libby scooted forward, leveraging herself along with that cast-heavy leg.

"Hang on," she said. "This might be cool."

She gathered the remaining candy-colored chunks, lining up the pieces according to color until she had a rainbow, more or less. When she was satisfied, she called over to the little kids: "Hey, do you guys want to watch me draw?"

The kindergartners exchanged wary glances.

"Come *on*," Libby pressed. "I'll draw anything you want. I'm kind of good at it."

Curious, May leaned forward. May couldn't draw for squat, but she liked watching other people be good at things.

Slowly, the kindergartners emerged from their hiding places. One particularly bold child shouted, "Draw a dog!"

Libby obliged, producing a green dog with a yellow collar and big blue eyes. The kindergarten girl adjusted her glasses and stood on tiptoes, squinting to see all the way over to the drawing. She nodded and looked back at her classmates. "It's a good dog," she declared.

And in five seconds flat, a mob of demanding munchkins descended on Libby and May, each one yelling a request.

"Draw a cat!"

"A boat!"

"A horse!"

"Do a haunted house!" urged a curly-haired kid with untied shoelaces.

Libby grinned. "A haunted house . . . I like that one, yeah. May, give me some purple, would you?"

May paused, not because she objected to purple but because she was a little surprised. It was the first time anyone except her teacher had said her name at school. Finally, she replied, "Yeah, sure," even though it was hard to say "sure" without her Georgia accent coming through.

She handed over the chalk and watched as Libby spent the next few minutes drawing something right out of a scary movie — except it was sort of cute instead of frightening. The house's shape was cartoony, and behind the broken windows, all the ghosts were smiling.

A boy in a Mariners baseball shirt stomped up to the finished drawing and assessed it with a critical eye. "Now you have to draw a princess who lives there!"

"A princess who lives in the haunted house. Got it." Libby reached for the yellow, pink, and red nubs of chalk. Soon, a figure took shape — a blue-haired girl in a puff-sleeved princess dress, wearing a big gold crown and red sneakers.

May was transfixed. She'd never seen anybody draw anything half so good, at least not since that time at Six Flags, when a guy at a booth drew her picture for ten bucks. When Libby was finished, the little boy in the baseball shirt said the princess was awesome, and everyone agreed. Especially May.

But then the boy said, "Wait, it's not done. You forgot her wand. Give her a magic wand."

May shook her head. "Nah, Libby," she said, forgetting her accent for once. "Don't give her a wand. Anyone can be awesome with magic. You should give her something cool instead."

"Something cool, okay. Like . . . what?"

"Ooh!" she exclaimed. "Give her a sword!"

"A sword! Yeah . . ." Libby took the purple chalk and swept it along the concrete. "A sword takes *skill*." When she was done, she put the chalk down and wiped her hands on her pants. "How about that?"

"The sword looks kind of weird . . . ?" May said. She had forgotten about the kindergartners too.

"It's a katana sword. Like the kind ninjas use. They're basically the best swords ever."

"Oh yeah, right," May said, pretending she knew all about ninjas. "You can really mess somebody up with one of *those*."

"Now we just have to give her a name. . . ." Libby looked up. "May? You got any ideas?"

May pondered the question. She needed a good answer. She might have a new friend in the works, and she didn't want to blow it.

"If she's got a sword, she's probably on a mission," she said. "Maybe she's a spy, or a soldier, or like you said — she could be a ninja. She could have a code name." It couldn't be too complicated. It should be easy to remember, and quick off the tongue. "We could call her . . . Princess X."

"Why X?" Libby asked.

"Because *X* is the most mysterious letter," May told her. "And things with X's in them are usually pretty cool." She hoped she was right, and it was cool enough.

Libby considered this, and then nodded. "Okay. That works for me!"

May exhaled and smiled. "I'm glad you like it."

"I *do* like it," Libby replied as she added the final touches. The glimmer on the princess's crown. The logo on her Chucks. "It'll work just fine. So here she is — I give you: Princess X!"

I AM PRINCESS X.

THIS IS MY HOUSE. IT IS HAUNTED, BUT I LOVE IT ANYWAY.

ALL THE GHOSTS ARE VERY NICE.

WE ARE ALL GOOD FRIENDS.

I RULE A KINGDOM CALLED **SILVERDALE** ALL BY MYSELF

THE PAINTED DESERT

RIVER PARK FARMS

CLOUDLAND MOUNTAINS

CAPITAL TOWN

SWAMP OF MEMORIES

MY HOUSE

MY PARENTS AREN'T DEAD OR ANYTHING

IT'S A LOT OF WORK BEING THE PRINCESS, BUT IT'S MOSTLY FUN.

THEY'RE JUST RETIRED.

Libby and May did not leave Princess X on the sidewalk. They took her home, and together, they built an imaginary empire. The princess's haunted house sat atop a hill, surrounded by an impenetrable iron fence as thick as a labyrinth hedge. From there she fought monsters, ghosts, and other unsavory invaders wherever she encountered them.

May wrote a lot, Libby drew a lot, and by their last year of middle school, they'd created an entire library dedicated to Princess X. The stories filled big, fat notebooks, huge spiral sketchbooks, shoe boxes, crates, and reusable grocery bags. They archived this vast collection at Libby's house. Libby's dad was an engineer at Microsoft, and they had a house not far from "Millionaire's Row," so she had a big bedroom with a big closet, and that's where everything went.

May lived with her parents in a small apartment, in an old building from back when a bedroom held nothing but a bed. She was always the shortest one in the class, always cheaply dressed, with straight brown hair and thick-lensed glasses that she hated. When she got teased about them, she said they were so strong she could see into the future, and the power persisted even after she traded the glasses for contacts.

Libby, on the other hand, looked like a Forever 21 model by the time she was twelve. She wore dangling earrings and designer jeans, and she was naturally cool, so cool she told everyone her grandma was a ninja, and everyone believed her. Except that Libby's own mom came from Japan and said there weren't any ninjas anymore. She also said the *real* reason Libby's grandmother never came to visit was Libby's dad, since he wasn't from Japan. He was born someplace else — wherever white people come from — and there wasn't much Libby could do about that.

So she drew a lot of stories about ninjas because she *could* do something about ninjas. Probably. If she ever met any.

Neither May nor Libby ever quite made any other good friends, because they didn't *need* any other good friends. They played a lot of video games, read a lot of comics, watched a lot of TV, and ate a lot of junk food. They climbed on the troll statue out in Fremont, taking selfies under the neon artwork of ballroom dancers, rocket ships, and diving ladies in old-fashioned swimming caps. They did each other's homework and sat up late with flashlights under the covers, downloading dirty books onto Libby's e-reader and giggling madly until they got caught. They spent their allowances on arm warmers, magazines, and hot chocolate at their favorite local joint, Black Tazza — pretending it was coffee so they could feel like grown-ups. But even with all the regular real-life stuff, they still found time for Princess X, dragging their binders to the coffee shop and spreading out their notes, making up character sheets for all the good guys, bad guys, and other assorted guys who populated the country of Silverdale. The princess became their alter ego, their avatar, their third best friend.

One day, on the sidewalk in front of Pacific Place mall, Libby got hollered at by a wild-eyed white guy with a crazy sign that listed all the reasons America was going to hell. The sign was particularly concerned about how everyone was marrying everyone else, and soon America wouldn't have any black, white, yellow, or red people anymore — just gray ones.

May called the sign waver stupid and said, "Anyway, gray's a great color — especially in Seattle. Around here, gray's practically patriotic."

"Heck, yeah, gray's a great color," Libby said, mustering a smile. "Just look at me: I make gray look *cool*."

A few weeks after that, they took a standardized test at school. One of the questions asked for the student's race, and Libby wrote in *gray* next to the line that came after *other*.

The teacher gave her a fresh sheet and made her do that part over. He said that when Libby grew up, she could call herself anything she wanted; but on that test, she'd have to pick one of the ovals and fill it in, even if it wasn't quite right.

But of course, Libby didn't grow up. She died in Salmon Bay instead. Supposedly.

Mrs. Deaton fell asleep while she was driving Libby home from gymnastics. She drove off the Ballard Bridge, and it took the search-and-rescue people two days to find the car. When they did, Mrs. Deaton's body was still strapped into the driver's seat, but Libby was missing. Her backpack was lying on the floor on the passenger side, and her window was broken out.

For years, May would dream that Libby had escaped — that she'd somehow kicked free of the sinking car and clawed her way to the surface through the night-black water, cold as a soda from the fridge, the city lights sparkling above her like stars. Leading her up. Leading her out. She'd burst through the surface of the Bay, her soaked hair spilling down her shoulders like a mermaid's, trailing behind her as she swam toward home.

And then May always woke up cold and crying, because that wasn't what happened at all.

What happened was, they found Libby's body a couple weeks later, slapping slowly, squishily against a sailboat at a nearby marina. She was half-destroyed by the nibbles of sea creatures, and swollen with water, unrecognizable to anyone. She was identified by her clothes and the soggy student ID in her back pocket.

If they'd only let her *see* Libby's body, May might have never had those dreams, she thought. She might've never picked up her old glasses, wearing them to bed at night in case she could see something better than the future — she could see the past too. If she'd only gotten a glimpse of what was left of her best friend, her imagination wouldn't have lied with that same stupid dream of Libby's escape, over and over again, year after year.

Sometimes she'd go for a few months without it, and almost forget . . . and then the dream would sneak up on her, and she'd sit up shocked and shaking, so perfectly confident that she'd *seen* Libby, and she was *alive*, swimming to freedom. Swimming to May. Reaching for her outstretched hand. Almost grabbing it.

And then sinking back into Salmon Bay, because May didn't wear glasses anymore, and fortunes were just stories that weren't ever true in the first place.

*   *   *

There was a funeral — closed casket, natch. May tried to pry the coffin open when no one was looking, but they'd really locked that sucker down. Maybe everyone knew her better than she thought.

They buried Libby beside her mother in a distant suburb, so May couldn't visit her very often. The last time she went, she knew she probably wouldn't be back again anytime soon, or maybe ever. While her parents bickered quietly behind some tombstones and trees, May whispered to Libby as loudly as she dared.

"My parents are probably getting a divorce," she told her.

It felt weird to say it out loud, because her parents hadn't said it out loud yet. That didn't matter. She could see it coming from a mile away. She sat down cross-legged beside the grave, still lumpy and fresh, with just a smattering of new grass growing all scraggly over the top. She picked at the young, green blades, pulling them one by one and dropping them into a little pile.

"If they do get a divorce . . . or *when* they do, I guess . . . I'll probably have to go back to Atlanta with my mom." She barely breathed the words because she'd cry if they got any louder. "I'll have to go to a new school, and that's really going to freak me out. I don't know what I'll do if I have to share a locker with somebody else." She swallowed hard. "Our locker, yours and mine . . . it's just like you left it. Your dad never asked for any of your stuff back, so I just kept it there — I hope that's okay."

Libby's biology textbook with all her notes stuffed inside. Her gym clothes in a cotton bag, all lumpy where her sneakers were stuffed down inside it. Her water bottle. Her iPod.

"When school's out, I'll just take it all home with me. Not trying to steal your stuff." She let out a shaky little laugh that threatened to turn into a sob. "I just won't let anybody throw it away, that's all. I wish I could just leave it like it is, like, maybe put some kind of memorial plaque on it or something. . . ."

Her parents' voices got louder, and it didn't sound as though they were arguing anymore. Just talking, and coming back for May. On the one hand, she was annoyed. On the other hand, at least she didn't have to tell Libby about losing Princess X.

She wasn't sure she could say that part, even to a ghost. It was hard enough just to think about it.

It had happened like this: A week after the funeral, May's mom drove her over to the Deaton house one last time — but Mr. Deaton wasn't home. Nobody was there except the housekeeper, Anna, and she was wiping down bone-clean counters and sweeping prehistoric Cheerios out from under the refrigerator.

The place was empty. No furniture. Not even any curtains.

May ran past Anna up to Libby's old room and threw open the closet door, where their Princess X archive was kept.

"Sweetheart, I'm sorry," the housekeeper told her gently, once she'd caught up. "I'm sorry," she said again. "But everything's gone."

Mr. Deaton had quit his job, packed a suitcase, and set off for Michigan, where he'd grown up. He'd hired a company to empty the house in his wake, donating everything to Value Village or Goodwill. Then he'd tossed Anna the keys and told her to clean it up for the realtors. He wasn't coming back.

And neither was Princess X.

Frantic, May demanded that her mother shuttle her to every thrift store in King County, and she was loud and crazy enough that her mom obliged her. Or else her dad did, because that way her parents didn't have to spend any time together. They'd rather babysit their daughter through a nervous breakdown than face each other over supper.

May never did find those boxes filled with Princess X adventures, comic strips, and catalog cutouts of things the princess might wear or places she might go. Her parents never patched it up; they went ahead and split a few months later. Her dad stayed in Seattle, and her mom took her to live in Atlanta most of the year, with summer and alternating holidays back in the Northwest — so her accent got Southern again, and she was often cold and lonely.

Libby was dead. Princess X disappeared.

May lost her best friend again, and again, and again.

TWO

Three years passed.

And then there was a sticker.

May saw it on Broadway, in the corner of a shop window that would be demolished within days. The store was already empty — cleaned out and picked bare, with nothing left inside but dust bunnies and spiders. Everything was shuttered because the city was making way for a light rail station on Capitol Hill.

Every year when May returned for the summer, things were different like that. Sometimes it was a small boutique or coffee shop different, like when Black Tazza had closed during the spring. Sometimes it was a whole neighborhood different, like how these buildings would all be gone in a week.

That August, she'd be turning seventeen — so things were about to get *really* different. Or so she assumed. That's what everyone always said, at any rate.

But that first day in June, she saw the sticker on the bottom right corner of the soon-to-be-torn-down shop window.

She was on her way back from the University District, where she'd been camping out in a park with her notebook — plotting a novel she hadn't told anyone about, and waiting for her dad to notice she was gone. Her dad worked a lot, but sometimes he did it from home, not his office downtown. Even when he was home, it usually took him a few hours to look up and see that she wasn't there anymore. They got along all right, but that was mostly because they didn't spend much time together. May thought maybe she reminded him of her mother. She didn't take it too personally.

Anyway, she had a key to the apartment, and she came and went as she chose, to and from the thrift stores, bubble tea shops, and coffee-houses, where she still got hot chocolate instead of coffee. Her memories of Libby still stung sometimes, but she hung on to them. She might as well. The whole city was haunted by her.

So the sticker on the very last building before Olive Street shouldn't have caught her eye at all. It was vinyl, and cheap. The edge was starting to peel. The colors were a little faded. It was round with a black border.

But within this border was the outline of a girl with shiny blue hair. She wore a pink puff-sleeved dress, a tall gold crown, and red Chucks. In her left hand, she held a purple sword shaped like a katana.

All May could do was stand there staring at the sticker so hard that she couldn't see anything else. Her breath caught in her throat and she tried to choke it back down, but it stuck there like a big wad of gum. She tried to cough, and that worked a little better — except then she was crying: that dry-heaving cry where nothing comes out.

It didn't make any sense. It wasn't possible.

She reached out and touched the sticker anyway, barely believing it was real. It couldn't be, could it? She nudged her fingernail under the peeling edge, trying to pry it off in one piece — but it tore instead, and she was left holding the bottom half. The hem of a pink dress. The fire-engine-red shoes. The hand with a sword. Yes, it was *definitely* Princess X.

The rest of the sticker refused to budge, so she pulled out her phone and took a picture.

She kept staring at the stupid vinyl sticker like maybe it'd pop to life and tell her that none of it was ever true. Not the bridge. Not the car. Not the water. Not Libby's closed casket and her empty house, with an empty room, and an empty closet where the boxes of Princess X memorabilia used to be.

Maybe none of it *was* true. Or at least not the most important thing.

Maybe Libby was alive.

Her phone started to buzz. It was her dad. She didn't answer his call, because she had a feeling that her voice would sound like mud, and he'd want to know why. Instead, she put the phone away and walked slowly toward home, her mind reeling with a mix of confusion and excitement. What did the sticker mean? Did someone find their old notebooks, scavenged from some distant Value Village basement? Had someone from school decided to carry the torch? Was it just some bizarre, unlikely coincidence?

No. She didn't believe that last one for a minute. She didn't know what the sticker meant, but it meant *something*.

"There you are," her dad said when she came in the apartment door.

"Here I am," she confessed.

"I called."

"Sorry," she offered, but didn't explain. "You want to get some lunch?"

His shoulders lost some of their stiffness, and he relaxed into his usual slouch. "Lunch would be great. What are you thinking?"

"Mexican," she said firmly. If she couldn't hold it together over Mexican food, she could always blame the tears on jalapeños.

They wandered around the corner to a mom-and-pop joint that knew them on sight, and they slid into their preferred booth. They ordered their usual, and played the small-talk game until their food arrived.

Once it did, he prodded at her.

"Nothing's *wrong*," May assured him around a mouthful of sour cream and beans, but she didn't look at him when she said it.

"I didn't ask what was *wrong*. I asked what was *up*. You're . . . spacey. And you've used all the extra napkins to blow your nose."

She thought about lying. He would've liked it if she lied — if she could tell him something minor and dumb that wouldn't inconvenience him. But May was a terrible liar, and she didn't think it'd matter if she told him the truth. If it made him uncomfortable, well, *fine*. It made her uncomfortable too.

"All right, if you *really* want to know . . ." she began slowly. "It's about Libby."

He got quiet for a second. "What about her?"

May laughed, and she wasn't sure why. It hurt a little. "Okay, you remember that thing we used to work on? Princess X?"

"It'd be hard to forget her. You made me and your mother drive all over town, trying to find those boxes."

"Of course I did. They were important. I wanted them back."

Things went awkward and silent until he said, "Sorry," and looked down at his plate.

"It wasn't your fault we didn't find them," May said quickly.

"It was nobody's fault, I guess. But you know, for a while after you and your mom left, every now and again I'd walk by a secondhand shop and stick my head inside. Just in case they'd turned up."

"You . . . you did?" She was surprised and touched, but she wasn't sure how to tell him that, so she didn't.

He grinned. "You beat the habit into me." He took another big bite of burrito.

"But you never found them, or you would've said something." It was more a statement than a question. "So it would be *really weird* if Princess X turned up someplace now, right?"

He stopped chewing. Swallowed. Took the last napkin off the table and dabbed at his mouth without ever taking his eyes off May. "Turned up . . . where?"

"On a window, down on Broadway. There was a sticker."

"I assume you took a picture of this sticker. Show me." He gestured with his fork.

She dredged her phone up out of her bag. Her hands shook while she loaded the image. "Here," she said as she handed it to him.

Her dad squinted down at the small screen. "I'd say that's only half a sticker."

"I know. I tried to pull the sticker off first, but I ripped it. Here's the other half."

Despite her best efforts, the sticker had contorted itself into a cigarette-size tube of unwieldy stickiness. She forcibly unrolled it and smeared her palm across it, struggling to make it lie flat. It stuck to the plastic tablecloth, but tried to curl up again the moment her hand was out of the way.

Her dad held the phone next to the sticker, mentally mapping them into a single image. He cocked his head to the left, then the right. "That *is* weird."

"Weird? It's *impossible*."

"I wouldn't say that. *We* didn't find the boxes, but someone else might have. Maybe some kid picked them up someplace and thought it looked cool."

May slid down lower into the booth, the last bites of her enchilada grown cold. "I doubt it."

"You don't doubt it," he said. "You don't want to believe it, and that's not the same thing."

Her eyes were watering again. She fought them for control of her face, and mostly won. "Oh yeah?"

He sighed. "I know you want to believe that Libby's still out there someplace, drawing Princess X. But whatever this sticker means, that's not it. I'm sorry, I really am."

She wanted to be mad at him, but it could've been worse. She could've been trying to explain everything to her mom, and what a wreck *that* would have been. Her mom would have laughed and said she was wrong about the sticker. Then she'd go back to playing Internet Scrabble, and May would get so mad that she'd launch into another ugly cry, and they'd fight, and May would hate her for lying about something so obvious, and not even caring about it.

At least her dad didn't tell her she was an idiot. He didn't always get her, but he never dismissed her out of hand. He took everything seriously, which was great sometimes. But at that moment, May wanted the fairy tale, and if that's what she wanted, he wasn't the guy to talk to.

So they quit talking about it. And once they got home, they watched the Venture Bros. on Netflix. Episode after episode, until her dad announced that it was bedtime and turned off the TV. That's how he always preferred to change the subject: with a remote control.

THREE

Over the next couple of days, May saw the princess everywhere.

The one on the window, that was the first. One slapped on a stop sign. One on the side of a public mailbox. One nearly eroded from a sidewalk; it'd definitely been there awhile. One on the side of a city bus. And then she had to start making note of the graffiti too, because someone's Princess X stencil saw a whole lot of action downtown. May found the artwork next to the storm runoff drains. Down at the Pike Place Market, beside the big brass pig across from the fish-flinging guys who always end up on postcards. Beside the world's first Starbucks, which was brighter and more packed with tourists than Starbucks tend to be anyplace else.

The quest for Princess X became a scavenger hunt. Every time she found an image, she snapped a picture and then asked anyone nearby — any shop workers or stall merchants, anyone who might linger from day to day — if they knew what it meant, or if they'd seen who put the image there.

The answer was always no, no, no.

May stalked the streets in sunglasses and earbuds, even when the sun wasn't out and there was no music playing on her iPod, just so no one would talk to her, and she could hunt for Princess X without being bothered. She moved through the city like a spy, watching and listening without being seen or heard. She'd never had a problem being invisible, especially when she and Libby were together. Everyone had always looked at Libby.

She kept her eyes peeled for graffiti artists and punks, watching for anyone who might be the sort to slap stickers on public property. She watched the skater kids and the cosplay girls, the students at bus stops, and the little grade-school goons with lunch boxes.

And without meaning to, she kind of watched for Libby. Some part of her wondered if she wouldn't find more evidence of Princess X lurking in the spots the two of them had spent the most time together, and it gave her an excuse to visit their old stomping grounds. May didn't expect to just chase the stickers straight to Libby's ghost or anything. She just stopped avoiding their favorite places, that was all. She hadn't even realized she'd been doing it, but it was true — she had always stayed away from their old hangouts, taking the long way around.

But not anymore.

Their favorite bookstore had closed, and then turned into a record store . . . and then that had closed too, but the storefront was still there. May thought of the rack of comics that used to be in the back, where Libby flipped through the books endlessly, looking for any artwork cool enough to copy.

"Copying is the sincerest form of flattery," May used to tell her.

She could still hear Libby's voice, clear as a bell from three years away: "It's also really good practice."

She already knew Black Tazza wasn't open anymore, so there was no point in visiting it. She checked out the old Walgreens where, once upon a time, she and Libby used to shop for lip gloss and nail polish while they waited for the bus. There was always time to try one more swipe of lipstick across the back of their hands, testing to see if it'd look good against their skin. There was always room for one more sweep of pearl pink, candy apple, or cinnamon blush.

She didn't see any of those colors anymore, but she saw two other girls giggling and spreading lip gloss wands over their wrists, arguing over what looked better. Instead of getting teary, she went ahead and smiled.

Outside on the bus stop sign, someone had slapped a Princess X sticker. That made her smile too.

Finally, two whole days after discovering the sticker on Broadway, she caught a break.

She was sitting in Volunteer Park at the edge of a pond, next to a fake great blue heron — a statue that hypothetically scared away the real ones so they wouldn't eat the koi. She had opened her notebook and turned to the notes for her novel in progress, but she couldn't concentrate enough to do much more than doodle in the margins. There was too much else on her mind, and really, all she wanted to do was sit down and write some Princess X stories.

It had taken awhile to learn how to write by herself, without someone to sketch out the pictures she described. It was a lot harder to tell stories without a friend, and with just the words to work with — because May never could draw for crap, and she never did get much better than crap. But once she figured out a few things, writing came easy. Ideas had always been her strong suit. Now it was just a matter of getting them down on paper.

She looked up at the enormous brick water tower behind her and tried to see it as something other than a turret in Princess X's haunted house. It was part of a castle instead — or a prison where the worst of the worst were locked up for life.

Then a guy with a skateboard came shooting toward her so fast that she had to jerk her feet out of the way. With a rattling clatter of asphalt-chewed wheels, he passed her by and continued up to the overlook, where a big round sculpture called the Black Sun framed the Space Needle on a clear day.

She scowled after him. But then fading into the distance, on the back of his bag, she saw a familiar logo. It bobbed and bounced as he kicked up the board, and vanished as he set the bag aside. He dropped himself onto the edge of the sculpture's big platform, pulled out a pack of cigarettes, and sparked one up.

Before May even knew what she was doing, she'd picked up her own bag — a beat-up canvas messenger with an octopus on it — and slung it across her chest. She strolled toward the skater, but she'd gotten so good at being invisible that he didn't see her until she was standing right in front of him, blocking his view of the reservoir.

He looked her up and down without any menace or even appraisal. She thought maybe he was trying to make her step aside, using the power of his brain.

She didn't move. She just said, "Hey."

"Hey," he said right back at her, without blinking. He was about her own age, give or take a couple of years in either direction, with scraped-up elbows and holes in the knees of his jeans.

"Can I ask you something?"

"Go for it."

She nudged his bag with her shoe. "That sticker . . ." she said, but when he turned the bag around, she realized she'd been mistaken. "That patch, I mean. Where did you get it?"

He jabbed it with his finger. "This one? My girlfriend got it for me."

"Okay, then where'd *she* get it?"

He shrugged. "The website, I guess. You can get stickers, patches, all that kind of stuff. Why? Are you a fan?"

She swallowed hard. "Of the . . . website?"

"Okay, I guess not. You got a pen?"

She dug one out of her bag and handed it to him. He grabbed her hand and turned it over so her palm faced up. Across it he scrawled:

www.iamprincessX.com

She read the URL over and over again, choking on it.

"Thanks," she managed to say as she stepped away from him and started back down the hill.

It wasn't just her wacky imagination, not somebody's cute cartoon with a coincidental resemblance, not a bad case of nostalgia showing her what she wanted to see. It was Princess X. *Her* Princess X. *Libby's* Princess X. It was on the Internet, and that meant it was *real*.

May shook her phone as though she could intimidate more battery life into it, and of course she couldn't. But she was only a few blocks from her dad's apartment, so she ran all the way there. She sweated through her T-shirt and sweater, which was a very attractive look, she was sure — but she made it home, let herself inside, then slammed the door shut and dashed for her bedroom. She grabbed her laptop and dragged it into the living room, where the wireless connection was strongest, and waited what felt like forever for the machine to boot up.

"Dad?" she called out. It had only just occurred to her that he might be home. But he didn't answer, and that meant he wasn't working from the back room today. Good. She wanted some privacy.

Her browser popped up, and she plugged in the URL that she already knew by heart. She wormed herself out of the damp sweater and threw it on the floor, then grabbed a throw from the back of the couch and wrapped it around her shoulders like a shawl.

IAmPrincessX.com.

There it was.

May took a deep breath and let it out again, measured and slow.

The website was mostly done in black and gray with pink and red accents, achieving a surprisingly dark look for a story about a blue-haired princess in a puffy dress. May dragged the cursor around — it wasn't an ordinary arrow, but a tiny purple sword! She loved it! — and examined the page pixel by pixel.

Beneath the banner was a large shot of the princess with her sword, flanked by the ghost of a woman on one side, and a slender, brown-haired man on the other. The woman was sad and ethereal, trailing ectoplasm and tears, with seaweed in her hair and blood pouring down the front of her dress. The man was small-eyed and angry, with too-long, knobby limbs and grasping fingers that had too many knuckles.

And the princess herself . . . she was no simple cartoon anymore, but a fully fledged character. She had wild black hair with electric blue streaks, and her mouth was set in a determined line. She looked very much like May imagined Libby might, had she lived to see high school. Tough and pretty. Slim and tall. Ready to kick some butt.

At first, May thought the page was static, but when she noodled with the cursor, drawing it over here, over there — she discovered Easter eggs hidden in the images. The ghost's bloody chest wound revealed hover text that read, SHE DROVE FOR AS LONG AS SHE COULD. In the same way, the man's right hand declared, PINS AND NEEDLES, PALMS AND KNIVES. The princess's katana sword urged May, FIND THE FOUR KEYS.

At the bottom of the page, a long thread of water flowed. It must be some kind of animated GIF, she assumed; but when she hovered the cursor over it, it made little splashes — and a warm gold highlight told her that this was a link.

She double-clicked it.

THE
GHOST
QUEEN

MOTHER AND AVENGING SPIRIT, the Ghost Queen was flung into the ocean but did not drown. Her life and her child were taken away. She will not fade or forget. Advisor and protector, friend and oracle. Her wisdom and magic hide the princess from the Needle Man.

PRINCESS X

THE PRINCESS fell into the water twice. The first time, the Needle Man lifted her out from the waves and carried her home. He wished to build a new child out of her blood and bones, but she fled before he could reshape her. She ran, guarded by her mother's spirit, and now they walk together through an unnamed land, seeking safety, freedom, and justice.

THE
NEEDLE
MAN

A SAD KING from a foreign land. His daughter was lost and he was alone, so he captured Princess X and brought her to live in his castle. But the princess refused to love him — and she escaped one night in a storm. Now the Needle Man hunts the princess night and day. He must find her and kill her before she learns the secret of the Four Keys.

THE
FOUR
KEYS

A SERIES OF MAGICAL OBJECTS shrouded in mystery and hidden by ancient wizards. When combined, these four keys form a powerful spell that will vanquish the Needle Man, freeing the princess and her mother forever.

The sword cursor followed May's train of thought, roaming across the pictures and the text. Except for Princess X herself, none of this was right. These were not May's stories. This was not anything she and Libby had negotiated under the covers after bedtime, flashlights and markers scattered around on the sheets. There was no mention of the city of Silverdale or the haunted house high up on a hill where the princess watched out over the city — fighting any and all crime she spied below.

Except . . .

Except the Ghost Queen bore a *crazy* resemblance to Mrs. Deaton. Even if May could overlook Princess X's similarity to Libby (and she *couldn't*), the Ghost Queen was no case of coincidence. No way. She was even flung into the ocean, just like the real woman. Sort of.

But who was this Needle Man?

She pushed the cursor over to his profile, hunting a link to tell her more. But nothing highlighted, illuminated, or otherwise suggested there was further content to be found.

Then she tried the Four Keys — which were illustrated by four long, old-fashioned keys tied together with a red ribbon. She discovered a link buried in the ribbon's bow, so she clicked it to see where it would take her.

WHAT DID YOU FIND IN
THE FIRE, PRINCESS X?

I FOUND A GOLD MASK
WITH SECRETS IN ITS EYES.

WHAT DID YOU FIND IN THE
SKY, PRINCESS X?

I FOUND A RED BOX MADE OF
LIGHTNING AND GLASS.

WHAT DID YOU FIND IN THE
GROUND, PRINCESS X?

I FOUND A BLACK MIRROR
THAT SANG ABOUT THE SUN.

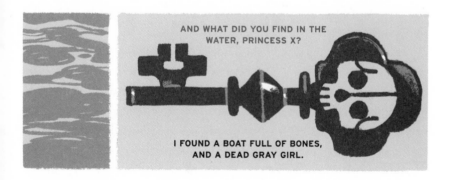

AND WHAT DID YOU FIND IN THE
WATER, PRINCESS X?

I FOUND A BOAT FULL OF BONES,
AND A DEAD GRAY GIRL.

May clapped her hand over her mouth to keep in her scream.

FOUR

May's heart raced and her hands shook as she brushed her fingers across the touch pad, highlighting that last line. "Gray girl" could mean only one thing, one person. It could mean only Libby.

She right-clicked on the main page, which gave her a look at the website's source code. The code didn't tell her much; she recognized CSS when she saw it, but it didn't mean anything to her. Her baby-step HTML couldn't code anything more complicated than fonts, tables, and pictures. So that was a bust.

Then she backtracked out of the tricky stuff and went straight to the source of all knowledge: She googled half a dozen variations on *Princess X*. And that's when she learned exactly how late she was to the party. Her throat was dry, but this was no time for a soda, not when a dozen pages of links presented themselves. Right down the line, she clicked and clicked and clicked, until she had so many tabs open that they mushed together on her header bar.

May found a CafePress site chock-full of messenger bags, coffee mugs, and posters with Princess X art . . . but a closer inspection revealed that it was "unofficial" gear. No connection to the original website was claimed or implied, according to the very careful wording on the account information page. Next she found about a dozen DeviantArt listings for fan-made pictures and stories. And in the comments, when she went scrolling down beneath the artwork, she found a lot of useful information.

Or rather, she learned that nobody had any useful information, which was still (in its own funny way) useful information. Nobody knew who drew or produced the Princess X website, nobody knew who wrote the comics . . . and everybody *wanted* to know.

Reddit really drove the mystery home. There, she found three different subreddits with an assortment of conspiracy theories, each one proposing One True Identity for the Princess X creator, who had mysteriously burst onto the scene about six months ago, producing the hottest, most mysterious, most widely followed webcomic since *Penny Arcade*. May didn't know what *Penny Arcade* was, either — so when she saw several redditors make that comparison, she didn't feel quite so bad for not having heard of the *Princess X* comic.

"I've *got* to spend more time on the Internet," she muttered to herself, and she kept on reading.

None of the Reddit theories were very interesting. Two were completely crazy, unless there was any truth to time-traveling or fairies; two others proposed that famous writers were using the site to play around anonymously; one claimed to actually *be* the author — but of course, that poster also claimed to have been hired to murder Bigfoot, so whatever; and one got her attention for about five seconds because it suggested that the webcomic was dictated by a ghost.

But then it got stupid. According to this particular theory, it wasn't an *interesting* ghost. Certainly not the ghost of Libby. In short, some dude thought it must be the ghost of an old man who'd been found dead in his house, mummified about ten years ago. He had pictures of the guy and everything, but they could've been pictures of any old dead guy in any old house, and May didn't know exactly what the pictures did to back him up.

When all was said and done, the Internet gave her a lot of speculation, some nutty ideas, and a bunch of people mooching off the webcomic, since no one had come forward to claim the merchandising rights. Apparently, anyone with a Zazzle account could whip up whatever Princess X stuff they liked, and turn a profit.

For a minute or two, May wondered if *she* could make any claim to the rights. She hadn't drawn Princess X, no — but she had written the original adventures, not that she could prove it. She hadn't written anything on the website, for that matter, so, well, maybe not. She still couldn't shake the annoying feeling that other people were making money on a private project — maybe even a whole fortune in stickers and shirts.

But that was kind of dumb, and she knew it. Surely no one really made a killing on stickers and shirts, and she didn't want money from *Princess X*: She wanted *answers*. She wanted to know who was writing it, because she knew — she knew, at the bottom of her soul — that it *couldn't* be anyone but Libby.

She spent another half hour surfing around, but the only really cool thing she turned up was a set of pictures taken at San Diego Comic-Con, where three friends had dressed up as Princess X, the Ghost Queen, and the Needle Man. The costumes were great — absolutely dead-on — but the girl dressed as the princess looked nothing like Libby. May couldn't decide if that made her happy or sad.

She was running out of Internet corners to poke with a stick, so she gave up and went back to IAmPrincessX.com . . . and only then did she notice she'd kind of been avoiding it. She was obsessed with it, but she could barely bring herself to look at it. She wanted answers, of course. *Obviously*. But if she found those answers, she might not like them.

Now there it was again: the lovely main page with the cool sword icon and burbling water animation. And there, in the upper right corner, two options: (1) Most Recent Comic, and (2) Read from the Beginning.

She clicked READ FROM THE BEGINNING, and came up with a page whose dated URL said it'd been posted around New Year's.

And she started to read.

THEY SAID THERE WAS NO CURE AND NO HOPE.

THE CURSE WAS IN HER BLOOD. IN HER BONES.

SO HE SEARCHED FOR BETTER BLOOD. BETTER BONES.

HE FOUND A VERY GOOD MATCH.

HE FOUND THE PRINCESS.

BUT HER PARENTS REFUSED HIM.

HE CHOSE TO DEFY THEM.

HE WAITED AS LONG
AS HE COULD.

HE WAITED UNTIL THERE
WAS NO TIME TO ASK.
ONLY TIME TO TAKE.

BANG

SCREEE

May sat there for a minute, just letting that sink in.

Never mind that the girls in the third panel were playing with side-walk chalk — the dark-haired one was *clearly* Princess X in normal kid clothes. And the princess's friend was a brown-haired girl wearing a T-shirt with a LOLcat on it. She remembered that shirt. Libby had had a matching one, so May still had hers someplace, folded up in the back of her closet in Atlanta. It was way too small, but she'd never thrown it out. She couldn't, not after Libby had gone — and taken everything with her.

May licked her lips. She wanted a Coke, but she was too transfixed to get up and scare one out of the refrigerator. She squinted hard at the backgrounds, the clothes, the colors, trying to Sherlock any additional details from the artwork. There wasn't much to see. All the focus was on the characters, in close-up as often as not. The cars could've been any cars. The parking lot could've been any parking lot. The gun could've been any gun.

But the girls . . . *they* were Libby and May. Anyone who ever met the pair of them could see it at a glance, and it thrilled her to see herself included in this new version of her old tales. There she was, plain as day. It meant something important that she was there. It was an invita-tion. It was encouragement. It was a hint that impossible things might not be so impossible after all — but that was a dangerous thing to think, wasn't it?

May squinted at the image of the injured woman and tried to remember Mrs. Deaton's haircut or clothing style, but her memory was even more vague than the lines on the screen. She mostly recalled a woman in her late thirties, with dark hair and a fondness for sheath dresses.

Regardless, the woman in the comic *had* to be Mrs. Deaton. It made perfect sense, except for the one obvious misstep: Mrs. Deaton was never shot. She drowned.

Supposedly.

A key made a little grinding sound in the front door's lock, announcing that May's dad was finally home from work.

"May, are you here?"

"Yeah," she yelled back, snapping the laptop shut before he could see it. She wrapped the blanket around herself so it was about as modest as a big bathrobe, and then, when he joined her in the living room, she dropped her voice to a normal volume. "Hey, let me ask you something."

He dropped himself into the recliner. "This sounds serious," he said with a nervous half smile.

"It's about Libby and her mom."

"Oh," he said carefully. "So you're still on that Princess X kick."

"Of *course* I'm still on that kick." She tried to keep from sounding irritated. She probably didn't do a great job of it. "And this is the part of the kick where I ask you about what went down when Mrs. Deaton drove off the bridge."

"You're not looking for stickers anymore?"

"No, I found more than that. So tell me how the Deatons died."

"They drowned," he said flatly. "You know that already."

And just like that, May knew he was lying. That blank, dead tone . . . that was his lying voice. It was the voice he used to hide what he was really thinking, or really feeling. May was a terrible liar too, but she was terrible in the other direction: She always got too emotional, too desperate to sell her story.

She said, "Yeah, but I want to talk about what *really* happened. Not what everyone *said* happened."

Her father squirmed. "You didn't need all the details, kiddo. God knows, I didn't need all the details. How they found her body, and it was all decomposed from being in the water . . ."

She snapped, "Not Libby!" She didn't want to hear any of that again, even if it turned out none of it was true. "I'm talking about her mom. She didn't drown, did she?"

"Yes, she did. She drove off the bridge and she drowned."

"But not before somebody *shot* her."

He opened his mouth to reply, but then his jaw jerked shut. He opened his mouth again and closed it. Whatever he'd been about to say, he started over with something else. "Where did you hear that? On the Internet?"

"Yes, on the Internet," she bluffed. It was basically true. And if she'd had enough time before he came home, she would've trolled for old news articles on the case. It had been three years since Libby and her mom died, but surely she'd find something archived *some*place.

Her dad sighed heavily and sank back into the recliner, like he was hoping it would just swallow him up. "You were bound to find out one of these days. I thought you'd get over it, and in time . . . it wouldn't matter so much anymore. But I guess this means it hasn't been long enough yet."

He misunderstood everything, and she kind of wanted to kick him for it — but she clamped it all down and clenched her fists. "God, you're such a *jerk*."

He sat forward, elbows on his knees. "Oh, I'm a jerk, really? Fine, if that's what you want to think, but someday you'll understand — we were only trying to protect you."

"*We?*"

"Your mother and I agreed that there were some things you just . . . you didn't need to hear. We knew you'd pick up bits and pieces, but what good would it do, letting you know they'd been murdered? For Christ's sake," he added, almost under his breath, "you were obsessive enough as it was."

"*That's* why you didn't let me go to her funeral." She meant Mrs. Deaton's funeral. Obviously, she'd gone to Libby's. "*That's* why you kept me away from the Internet, and kept the TV off. No local news . . ." That had been her mom's mantra in the weeks right after it happened. *No Internet. No TV. No local news.* And school had just gotten out, so she couldn't hear it from the other kids — not that they'd talked to her much anyway.

"It was for the best," her dad said weakly.

"You're liars. Both you *and* Mom," she concluded. She could feel her neck flushing warm just thinking about it. "Somebody killed them, and . . ." The next step only then occurred to her. "And they never caught who did it, did they?"

"No, they never caught him. Listen, kid . . ." He was being tired and sad again, but calling her kid was no way to worm back into her good graces. "We didn't want to give you nightmares. We didn't want you thinking there was somebody out there — somebody who might come for you next."

"I wouldn't have thought that. Jesus, Dad — I didn't even think of that until *just now*, thanks!"

"You were *grieving*. You were already making up stories about how it hadn't been real, and Libby wasn't dead. You kept talking about that dream you had all the time — about her swimming up . . ." His voice trailed away, then gathered strength again. "You wanted so badly to believe it was all a mistake, but it was worse than you knew, worse than an accident. So we did the only sane thing we could, and we left out the worst parts. It was too much to handle. For all of us."

She slammed back into the couch. "Oh, shut *up*." She glared at him hard enough to burn holes in his shirt. "Her murderer is out there, maybe murdering more people."

"Yes, he's still out there. But he's *always* been out there, ever since it happened. Nothing new has occurred. You've just learned a new piece of information, that's all."

"Nothing new? You call the Princess X sticker nothing new?"

She had him there, and they both knew it. He weaseled anyway. "It might be a coincidence."

"Five seconds on the Internet would tell you different," she informed him. "There's a website too." Even as she said it, she felt a wave of warm stupidity for not checking there sooner. She gathered up her blanket, climbed to her feet, and shoved her laptop under her arm. Its battery was almost dead again, and she needed to plug it in. "Now, if you'll excuse me, I've got some reading to do."

"Great," he said as she left the room. "Just great."

She estimated it'd be about fifteen minutes before he called her mom. Not because her mom would be any help, but because he didn't want to feel that he was the only person who didn't understand his daughter. It was the only thing her parents had in common anymore, and the only thing they talked about. When they talked, which wasn't very often.

But May couldn't make herself care. Like she said, she had some reading to do.

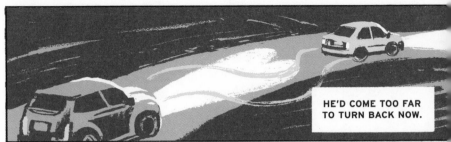

HE'D COME TOO FAR TO TURN BACK NOW.

THE MOTHER HAD LOST SO MUCH BLOOD . . . IT WAS ONLY A MATTER OF TIME.

ALL HE HAD TO DO WAS FOLLOW . . .

. . . AND WAIT

. . . AND SWIM.

FINALLY, HE HAD EVERYTHING HE NEEDED.

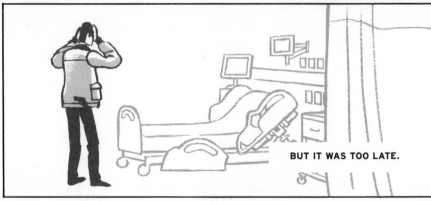

BUT IT WAS TOO LATE.

IT HAD ALL BEEN FOR NOTHING.

AND NOW HE HAD A VERY BIG PROBLEM.

May realized she was falling asleep.

She was exhausted and freaked out, and she had a headache from the tension between crying and trying not to cry. The laptop was warm on her legs, and her bed was soft underneath her. There was always tomorrow, because Libby was alive, out there, somewhere. She was alive today, and she'd be alive when May finally sorted through all the nonsense, lies, and background noise and could actually find her.

And she *would* find her.

After all, Libby had made it out alive, just like May dreamed. She swam up to the surface. She was pulled out of the water, into the car of the Needle Man — who wasn't always the Needle Man. Even the cadence of the story felt familiar. It felt like something they would've whispered together, behind the playground fort, passed by notes in class, or brainstormed out on the banks of Lake Union while they threw out bread crumbs for ducks.

It wasn't the beginning Libby and May had ever imagined. But then again, they'd never given the princess a beginning, had they? They'd only told her adventures going forward from the time she picked up her sword, fighting bad guys and monsters in her little red Chucks. They'd made up tales of daring and danger, but all those tales happened *after* she'd earned her name and her crown.

So this felt okay. It felt right.

And May didn't care if anyone else believed her, even her dad — the terrible liar, who only wanted to protect her. Or that's what he said, but he hadn't protected her from *squat*. All he'd done was hide the truth. And the truth shall set you free. She saw that someplace, a long time ago. Engraved on a ring. A line in a movie. A piece of dialogue from some play she didn't really remember very well.

The truth would set her free, all right. And it'd set Libby free too.

She would *make* it.

FIVE

The next morning, she flipped her laptop open, ready to begin reading again before she even considered breakfast . . . but the charger had fallen out and she hadn't closed it completely before crashing for the night, and now the battery was thoroughly, aggravatingly dead. She swore, scowled, and plugged it back in. Maybe she should get breakfast first after all.

Outside her bedroom, she found no sign of her father except a note on the fridge: *Got called in early. Sorry. We can talk tonight when I get home.*

The note implied he had a long workday ahead, which meant a long day of avoiding her. How convenient for them both. Maybe he'd done it on purpose.

But she didn't really want to talk to him anyway, and the note came with a twenty-dollar bill — stuck under a magnet shaped like a pug sitting on a box of chocolates — so it was hard to be *too* upset. She could eat like a king on twenty bucks, with hot chocolate money left over for tomorrow. The clock on the microwave said it was ten thirty, so it was still early enough to start the day with a muffin, or a bagel with toasty fixings; and by the time she got back home from the bagel shop, *surely* her laptop would be ready to roll.

She threw on some clothes and grabbed her messenger bag, then locked the door behind herself and took the slow elevator down to the lobby. Downstairs, pale morning sun spilled through the glass double doors that opened to the sidewalk.

She stopped by the bulletin board beside the mailboxes, because someone had put up a LOST CAT sign, and she was a sucker for those. Last summer, she'd returned two wayward felines to their homes, just by paying attention and having her cell phone ready. This poster's subject was a little black cat with big gold eyes, and the description said his name was Toby. She made a mental note of where Toby's owners lived, then the flyer right beside Toby's furry mug shot caught her attention.

Only one of the phone number strips remained, which implied that "Patrick's" services were in demand. On a whim, she snatched the last strip loose and stuffed it into her pocket along with her house key. If he was a student in need of a summer job, he was probably about her own age or a little older, and it might be worth asking him for help if she hit a dead end. After all, she was already running out of ideas for chasing down the website's host or creators.

She got her bagel and soda, ate it fast, and went back home. In her room, she sat on the bed, logged in to everything important, checked her email on the off chance she had any (which she didn't) . . . and went right back to IAmPrincessX.com.

She clicked to the place where she'd left off, on the page with the unnamed girl sitting against the wall, her shoulders hunched and her arms wrapped around her knees. But no matter where she moved the cursor or what she clicked on, nothing in the comic lit up to indicate a link, and nothing flashed a new address in the bottom information bar . . . so maybe she was overthinking it.

No. There *had* to be more.

But her laptop picked that page to crap out entirely.

She shook the computer like an Etch A Sketch, checked all the sensor lights, and couldn't conclude anything except that it wasn't working right that moment — and if she was really, really lucky, maybe she'd only fried the battery. The whole thing was black and silent.

She jammed her fist into her pocket and retrieved the scrap of paper from Patrick's flyer. It was warm and a little damp from sitting against her sweaty leg, but she could read it just fine. One by one, she dialed the digits.

SIX

Patrick Leander Hobbs had a problem. Several problems, really — but the worst problem was this: His parents believed that come fall semester, he was heading off to a dormitory on the University of Washington campus. They also thought that this impending relocation and four years of higher learning were entirely covered by a scholarship.

Neither one of these things was true.

Indeed, he'd earned a full-ride scholarship to the state university; it had been formally presented to him at graduation, just a few weeks previously. His parents had smiled and snapped photos with their phones, while the high school principal shook his hand and offered him a fancy envelope with the scholarship details inside.

Everyone was delighted, and no one was surprised. Patrick had *earned* that scholarship. His grades were superlative, his test scores nearly perfect, and his coding skills top-notch. He'd earned the endorsement of his computer science teachers across the board, and he'd even won a prestigious national contest for his web development prowess. As the president of the computer club proudly proclaimed, Patrick could MacGyver together a kick-ass site with nothing but a free WordPress template and a carton of Red Bull.

But a lot can change in a few weeks.

A lot *did* change.

For one thing, Patrick's girlfriend dumped him, the day after graduation. She did it with a text message, reading in its entirety: NOT COMING TO VCVR. GOING OUT W MIKE NOW. SRY.

In somewhat longer form, what Samantha meant was that she wouldn't be joining Patrick on his family vacation to Vancouver — due to the fact that she was now dating Michael Hannigan, who was really tall, okay, *fine*. But lots of people were tall, and this particular tall guy was so stupid he had three separate school-sponsored tutors to help him keep his grades above water. Michael Hannigan got such treatment because he was important to the football team. If he could pass with a C average, he'd become important to some university's sports program somewhere, and maybe, eventually, he'd make it to the NFL and earn a few million dollars a year for throwing a ball around and sustaining head injuries.

That's what happened to tall dumb guys, or that's what it looked like to Patrick.

Patrick was not tall, and he was not dumb.

He'd heard plenty of gossip that the security for public school record systems was total garbage, and a little long-distance poking at the firewall confirmed it for him. He slipped into the system, found the final grade reports for the junior class, and saw to it that one Samantha Elizabeth Peters lost a handful of percentage points on a couple of key finals.

It wasn't like he failed her out of school or anything. He just made sure she was assigned a couple of summer sessions for makeup. All he did was try to get her a better education. It was practically charity work.

However, the school's head of IT wasn't quite the idiot Patrick had hoped, and when she realized the firewall had been breached, it took her less than an hour to guess the culprit. It took her less than a day to *prove* the culprit, and about half that time to track the culprit down.

It took the Seattle Police Department five minutes to decide that charges weren't worth pursuing. But it took the University of Washington only an hour longer to decide they didn't need Patrick Hobbs in their STEM program that badly after all.

Somehow he managed to keep all of this information away from his mom and her boyfriend, with whom he lived at present. Luckily, both of them worked a lot. His mom was the manager of an Italian restaurant in the neighborhood, and her boyfriend repaired coffee roasting equipment and coffeemaking machines, so in the Pacific Northwest, he was always in high demand.

Patrick had just turned eighteen. It wasn't as if the authorities had any obligation to rat on him. All he had to do was get the mail and answer the apartment's old-fashioned landline if he wanted his secret kept. So by hook and crook, by treachery and outright lies, he successfully had his mother and her boyfriend convinced that all was well — and he'd be moving into a dormitory or frat house come September.

Which meant he had about eight weeks to pull something *amazing* out of his butt.

His butt was not being terribly helpful.

He had the idea of offering IT services, tech support, and that kind of thing — so he'd made up some flyers and posted them around, and he'd actually earned a few bucks that way. Almost a thousand bucks, in fact. It turned out people would pay just about anything to have viruses exterminated, along with the sketchy files that brought them on board in the first place. *Especially* when people didn't want their spouses or friends to find out about those files.

Still, it wasn't enough. Even if he kept up that pace all summer, another two thousand bucks would barely get him in the door of even the crappiest university. Even if he got a full-time job and did tech support on the side and ate nothing but ramen noodles and didn't buy any new video games until he was thirty, his summer earnings wouldn't cover an entry fee . . . much less tuition.

So Patrick Hobbs spent a lot of time thinking about money and how to get it. He also spent a lot of time on the Internet, entering contests, asking for recommendations and suggestions, and figuring out the hard way that the University of Washington's firewall was about a million times better than his high school's had ever been.

The clock was ticking and he was starting to sweat.

But then, the phone rang.

SEVEN

May listened as a guy's voice picked up on the other end of the phone: "Patrick Hobbs, IT consultant. How can I be of assistance?"

His voice said her guess was right, and he was about her age. "I need to consult somebody. About IT," she added lamely.

"And what is the nature of your difficulty?"

He didn't sound crisp and professional, but he sure was *trying* to sound crisp and professional. May couldn't decide if it was cute or annoying. She shifted the phone in her hand. "My computer died. Okay, maybe just the battery, I don't know — but I need it working again, and I probably need help with another thing too, and the other thing's more important. This may sound weird, but I need to find out who's behind a website."

"Ah. Are you experiencing some kind of harassment or bullying? Because if that's the case, you may want to take your concerns to the authorities."

"No. It's not like *that*."

"What?"

"It's . . . kind of a long story. So what are your rates? For IT consultation, you know."

"Forty bucks an hour."

"I have about . . ." She made a guess as to how much of her dad's twenty would be left over after supper and coffee. "Six-fifty."

"Sorry, sunshine. Trick's gotta eat."

May looked at her phone. Was this guy for real? "Did you . . . did you just call yourself *Trick*?"

"It's my name. Practically."

"It's only *part* of your name, dude," she conceded, none too gracefully. "What are you, in middle school or something?"

"College," he informed her.

"I doubt that," she said, still annoyed by the "sunshine."

"Well, you're wrong. I *am* in college. And it's still forty bucks an hour."

"Does anyone actually pay you that much? Ever?"

"All the time."

"Yeah, right."

"Spoken like someone who doesn't have a lot of porn on her computer."

"Well, okay. You've got me there," May admitted. "But can you help me find out who's behind this website?"

"Maybe, if you've got forty bucks an hour. What website are we talking about?"

"It's a webcomic called *Princess X.*"

He was quiet.

She said, "Hey, did you hear me? It's *Princess X,* and it's about —"

He cut her off. "It's about a princess with the red shoes and a sword, yeah, I know. But I can tell you right now, free of charge: *Nobody* knows who's behind it. It's one of the great mysteries of our time."

"Well, *I* know who's behind it. The girl who draws it used to be my best friend," she told him firmly. "And I can prove it."

"Seriously?"

No, not seriously . . . but it was too late to take it back now — and she had his interest, so she couldn't back down. "Yes, I can prove it. So are you on board or not? Six-fifty, that's all I have. But we can solve one of the great mysteries of our time, and that's *priceless.* Really, you ought to be paying *me* for this info, if the website's such a puzzle." She felt fired up now. "You can be the guy who breaks the story. You can be like that WikiLeaks guy. Or that guy who told the feds where to stick it, and hightailed it to China."

"I don't want to be either of those guys. Those guys are screwed."

"Then . . . then you can be like the white knights in Anonymous! Do you have a mask?"

"No."

"You might need a mask. You can buy one with six-fifty."

"You're *insane*."

"Oh, come on. Are you going to help, or what?"

He sighed. Heavily. With great drama. "Where are you?" he finally asked, like she'd worn him down and he was too tired to tell her no anymore.

"I'm on the third floor."

"I can come down, I guess."

"No." She stopped him there. "I'll meet you in the downstairs lobby, by the mailboxes. I'll bring my busted laptop. We can get coffee, and talk."

THE WORLD HAS ALREADY GIVEN UP ON HER.

THEY ARE BOTH ALONE NOW.

AND AFTER ALL,

SHE WAS A PERFECT MATCH.

OR SO HE THOUGHT.

HE HID HER ON AN ISLAND, LOCKED IN HIS HOUSE. AND EVERY DAY . . .

HE TOLD HER ABOUT THE FIRST PRINCESS, AND HOW SHE DIED.

BUT NOW HE AND THE NEW PRINCESS WERE A FAMILY. AND IF SHE'D ONLY GIVE HIM TIME . . .

SHE WOULD SURELY COME TO LOVE HIM.

SHE DOUBTED IT.

EIGHT

Trick met May in the lobby, as promised. She knew him at a glance.

He was only a little taller than her — making him short for a guy — and he was somewhat thin, with a long, narrow face that looked like it should've come with glasses, but didn't. He wore a short-sleeved shirt, unbuttoned over a black tee that advertised a band she didn't recognize. She rated him Kind Of Cute, in that "I'm quiet and I get good grades, but I'm secretly a badass" way that is either hot or ridiculous, depending on how much badass he was actually hiding. If any.

He said "Hey," and she said "Hey" back. The handshake was a little formal, but May took it in stride. "You're Trick?" she confirmed.

"And you're the girl who didn't give me a name, so . . . ?"

"May," she told him.

"And you're going to tell me who's behind *Princess X*?"

"*Maybe*. But first you have to fix my laptop. And then you have to help me reach her, or find her, or whatever. That's the deal, okay?"

"That's the deal," he promised.

They agreed to coffee, because everyone agrees to coffee in Seattle. From where they stood, there were no fewer than four Starbucks within easy walking distance, but they settled on an indie joint called Victrola because it was closest.

Victrola was busy, as usual. May ordered a mocha latte with extra chocolate, because chocolate made coffee tolerable, in her opinion — but she didn't want to look like too much of a wuss by going for her usual hot chocolate. Trick got a cup of drip, and added two sugars. They sat down on the bench seats by the front window, where all the cushions were mismatched, like everything else in Victrola.

Trick used his nose to nudge the red plastic stirring straw aside, and took a sip of his coffee. "So tell me about your friend. You think she invented *Princess X*? And now you can't find her?"

"Well, we both invented it, really. She drew the pictures, and I wrote the story — back in fifth grade. We kept it up until she supposedly died three years ago, but now that I've found this website, I *know* she's the one behind it. She's *definitely* not really dead."

"Sounds like wishful thinking to me."

"If I was going to wish Libby back to life, I sure wouldn't have her kidnapped and held hostage by some maniac who killed her mom. Have you read the comic?"

He pressed the edge of the thick white mug against his bottom lip. "I thought *everyone* had read it. It's crazy popular. Did you only just now find it?"

"The Internet is a big place. I can't read everything, everywhere, all the time," May grumbled. "I'd never heard of the website until a few days ago. I started seeing the stickers around town, and got curious."

"Only a few days ago? The merchandise has been making the rounds for months."

"Not in Atlanta."

"So that's what's up with the accent. I thought maybe you were faking it."

She scowled at him and took a sip of her mocha through the red stirring straw. "Maybe this was a bad idea."

"No!" he said, almost too loud, too fast. "No, look — you're right. I'm being a jerk, and I'm sorry. I want to hear about your friend, and I want to hear about the site. And I absolutely want to help solve the murder mystery, okay?"

It sounded enough like a promise, and she'd given him a name already — so she went ahead and told him everything else about Libby and her mom. She didn't really *mean* to, but once she got started, it all came tumbling out, and except for her dad, Trick was the only person she knew who had the slightest bit of interest in the subject. For that matter, he was the only other person she had to talk to, period. Everyone else she liked was either dead or back in Atlanta. Most of the kids she'd known from school in Seattle had moved away or moved on.

So whether it was a good idea or not, she told him about *her* Princess X — the one she and Libby made together, *not* the one that made it to the web — and how she'd hunted high and low for ages, trying to find those notebooks and shoe boxes of drawings. She told him about how she'd always thought Mrs. Deaton had drowned, but the comic suggested otherwise, and then her dad admitted that Libby's mom had been shot after all. When she finally finished talking, her mocha with extra chocolate was cold, and Trick's mug was empty, but he hadn't noticed.

"I know this sounds like some bizarre conspiracy theory," May said, leaning forward and setting her cup aside. "But you've gotta admit, there's something to it. It *can't* just be coincidence."

Carefully, and in a very calm, not-jerkish voice, he said, "You know, it's *possible* that someone found your notes and stuff, and just . . . went running away with the characters."

"*Technically*, anything is possible. But the Princess X and Ghost Mother characters even *look* like Libby and her mom. And I'm in it too, for a frame or two — before the girl becomes the princess." Before he could say anything else, she took an old-fashioned printed photo from her messenger bag. She'd grabbed it before leaving the apartment. It had been taken the day of a Jump Rope for Heart marathon. May and Libby were sweaty and beaming, and wearing matching oversize tees with the marathon's logo on it. Mrs. Deaton was standing behind them, a hand on each of their shoulders. "See?" she said, showing him the photo. "Libby looks just like the princess. It's *not* my imagination."

He examined the picture carefully, holding it by the edges as though it was some ancient artifact and he didn't want to mess it up. He nodded. "There's definitely some . . . yeah."

May took the photo back and stashed it away again. "She's out there, and she's behind this website. She's using it to ask for help, I think. She's looking for me."

"But if she's out there, and if she's looking for you" — May didn't like the "if" part, but he ignored her frown — "why wouldn't she just send you a message on Facebook? Find you on Tumblr, or Twitter? Surely you have an online profile *some*place?"

"Maybe she *can't*. If she's being held prisoner by this guy, maybe he's threatened her, told her he'd kill anyone who comes looking for her. Maybe she's using the website to protect me."

"You haven't gotten very far into the comic yet, have you?"

Her frown settled deeper. She hadn't even been lying, not really, but he'd still managed to bust her. "How can you tell?"

He shook his head. "Go home and keep reading. Princess X gets away from the Needle Man. Now she's on the run, collecting those four keys. Or that's where the story left off, last time I checked."

"Okay, fine: I only just started it. I've been clicking on all the images and looking for clues. It takes time."

"There's at least one fan forum you could check out. I forget the address, but you could google it in a second — thousands of people have been having a good old time, analyzing all the artwork and text. It might be worth reading. It'll give you an overview of the whole thing, anyway. You may find hints, if not clues."

"Yeah, those aren't the same thing," she groused, mostly to herself. She was irritated because now she was wondering about what he'd said a minute ago. If Libby had Internet access, well, May wasn't very hard to track down. She had Facebook, Twitter, and Vine accounts. She had a Tumblr too, though she was bad about updating it. "But it's *Libby*," she said, more quietly than she meant to. "I *know* it's her. I have to figure out how to help her. Maybe I'm the only one who *can*."

Patrick looked startled, as if she'd given him an idea. "See, what you just said there now . . . you might be right. If she wanted to, Libby could hide clues in plain sight in the comic — clues that no one would understand except for you." He leaned forward and tapped on the table to drive home his point. "Like, say you had a favorite ice-cream shop, or a favorite cartoon. A favorite boy band, something like that. Something that wouldn't mean anything to anybody else."

"We didn't listen to boy bands."

"All girls listen to boy bands at some point in their lives. It's a scientific fact. It's been true since the Beatles. Probably since *before* the Beatles."

May narrowed her eyes at him. "Well, aren't you just a fountain of knowledge. Nothing but scientific facts up there rattling around in your head."

"That's why you called me." He leaned back and twiddled his fingers thoughtfully. "Give me a little time, and I'll dive into some of the less, um, *obvious* places on the web. I'll ask around, call in a favor or two. And *you*," he said, squinting with one eye and pointing at her. "You go home and keep reading."

"I can't, remember? My laptop crapped out."

"Did you try turning it off and on again?"

She scowled, because she hadn't even tried and it was the most obvious thing ever — next to plugging it in and letting it charge. "I barely know you, and I already hate you."

"I'll take that as a no. Plug it in and let the battery fill up. Then try to reboot it, and let me know how that goes. I bet it'll work. It almost *always* works. Either way, we can meet up tomorrow and compare notes. Is two o'clock good for you?"

"What's special about two o'clock? You got something against breakfast?"

"I'll be up pretty late tonight, so I might not be out of bed before noon. I *love* breakfast." He grinned. "But geniuses always do their greatest work after dark. And you can bet I'm one of 'em."

MOTHER?

THE NEEDLE MAN'S KINGDOM IS BUILT ON SAND AND THE CORPSE OF HIS OWN CHILD, WHICH HE THREW INTO THE WATER.

YOU CAN ESCAPE HIM, BUT IT WILL TAKE COURAGE AND PATIENCE. I WILL HELP YOU.

SOON.

BUT TIME PASSES DIFFERENTLY FOR THE LIVING AND THE DEAD.

"SOON" CAN MEAN A MOMENT OR A LIFETIME.

SIX MONTHS. A YEAR.

TIME TO LEARN HOW TO WAIT.

TIME TO GROW. TIME TO REMEMBER.

TIME FOR A PRINCESS TO FIND A SWORD.

NINE

Back at home, deep in his personal Batcave, Trick went online.

This time, he was looking for trouble — or that's what his old computer science teacher would've said, if she'd known what he was up to. It was just as well that she didn't. Just as well she probably didn't know about the uglier Internet forums where money changed hands for various illegal activities, and she wasn't on 4chan (so far as he knew), and she surely wouldn't be familiar with the darknet. Or if she was, she'd probably deny it outright. It wasn't the kind of thing upstanding, respectable people went around crowing about.

Trick wasn't particularly upstanding or respectable, but he still didn't like the darknet. It was darker than even the name implied, so he stayed away from it as much as he could.

But that's where the really nasty, scary stuff went down — and the really useful, true, and terrible stuff too. So when he realized that the 4chan forum on the subject of Princess X had been taken over by fan-kids chatting about cosplay and sharing makeup tips, he went to the dark side anyway. It was the one place he knew for sure he'd find what he was looking for: an offer he'd seen a few months ago. Something that sounded so ridiculous that it had to be fake, except maybe it wasn't.

Maybe it was exactly what he needed.

Before he hit ENTER on the URL that would take him to the spot he wanted, he paused. Did he really want his needs met by the darknet? It was a deal with the devil, only worse than that. When you deal with the devil, you know what to expect. When you deal with the darknet, you don't have any idea who's doing the bargaining.

He hit ENTER anyway.

After all, he didn't have to agree to any deals if anybody offered him any. He was only there to look. He found the old post without too much trouble.

> Seeking the definitive whereabouts of the creator, artist, or web host for the Princess X website. Point me at the girl who makes this comic. Alert me to her location, or collect her and contact me. NO QUESTIONS ASKED. I know who she is, but I can't find her, and I know she has some heavy-duty help. Offering $100,000 to anyone who can put her into my hands. Wired directly to the bank account of your choice, anonymous if you prefer.

There wasn't much more to it than that. The guy was a stalker chasing jailbait at best, and a pedophile at worst. And whoever he was, he was web savvy enough to troll around the darknet as if he owned the place; his handle, XhunterM, turned up everywhere, so he might be a hacker — or he might be something worse.

Furthermore, he might not even *have* a hundred thousand dollars. There was no way to know for certain, and that was one of the dirtier tricks people played on places like the darknet. If you were bartering for something disgusting or illegal, you weren't likely to call the cops if you got cheated.

Trick felt gross just leaving the screen up, so he closed it and surfed back over to 4chan. That was only a *slightly* less stinky Internet armpit, but still a marginal improvement. Seeking yet further improvement, he clicked over to the Princess X reddit instead. He picked through the fan-kids, scrolling just to distract himself while pretending to do something useful, when he spotted a familiar handle.

There it was, yes. XhunterM.

His eyes narrowed thoughtfully. He wasn't about to engage the guy on the darknet — not on the creep's own turf — but maybe a reddit post wouldn't be too crazy. It wasn't really traceable, and his user ID didn't connect to any of his real-life personal details. As far as he knew.

Hey, *Princess X* fan — is that reward money still up for grabs?

He hit ENTER to post the message, and immediately his stomach dropped. This was a bad idea. It wasn't as though he was going to help May find her friend only to hand her over to some maybe-a-pedo. But a hundred grand was a lot of money, and he had a very bad need for a lot of money. Maybe there was some way to scam it loose. It wasn't wrong to scam creeps, right?

While he pondered the ethics and wisdom of this, he got a response, not even ninety seconds after he'd sent the message:

If you have any idea what's good for you, you'll forget the reward and everything to do with it.

The response didn't come from XhunterM. It came from some other handle, Sickbird3000. Intrigued, Trick hit the REPLY button.

HAT-TRICK9: Wrong handle. What'd you do, intercept the account? I don't want to talk to YOU.

SICKBIRD3000: Yes, I've stolen his account, and he can't log in to it anymore. Anyway, you really DON'T want to talk to him. Trust me.

HAT-TRICK9: I'm just curious about the money.

SICKBIRD3000: Your soul's worth a hundred grand?

HAT-TRICK9: I never said that. I just wondered if it was real.

SICKBIRD3000: Even if it is, don't touch it. You collect it, I'll take it away from you — and I'll make it hurt.

HAT-TRICK9: Is that a threat?

Trick refreshed the page for two minutes, but there was no response. Just as he was about to ask again, or maybe say something clever and threatening in return, the answer popped up.

> **SICKBIRD3000:** Yes, but let me be more clear, Hat-Trick. And that's a stupid pun, by the way. With half a dozen clicks, I know everything I need to know about you, Patrick Hobbs. You're broke and desperate, and almost in trouble with the law. You're a crappy hacker, or maybe you're just sloppy when you're jealous. I hope Samantha was worth losing that scholarship. I even feel sorry for you — so I hope you find some way to pay off UW in time to pretend nothing ever happened. But you're not going to do it this way. So take my response however you like — call it a threat, or call it friendly advice. But I don't want to see you sticking your nose into the site, the princess, or anything related to it.

Or . . . maybe Trick had been wrong about not having any of his personal info hooked up to his screen name. He swore under his breath. SickbirdWhatever must have had some kind of back door into his Internet service provider, or . . . or . . . something. An IP trace wasn't impossible, but it wasn't easy, either. The guy was either very crooked, or very good. Probably both. He was better than Trick, anyway, not that he had any plans to admit it.

And not that he'd let it scare him away from anything or anyone. Yet. He still had room to bluff, so he took it.

> **HAT-TRICK9:** Very impressive, you can chase down a handle. But if that's all you've got, you must not be the "heavy-duty help" the princess is supposedly getting.

> **SICKBIRD3000:** Yeah, I saw his post over there. Stay off the darknet, kid. The man behind that reward is a killer, and he'll

take down a dumb little h4x0r like you without thinking twice. If you don't believe me, and if you know even HALF of what you think you know, then you should ask yourself: What happened to Princess X's father? And then you should ask the Internet, and then you should shut up and pretend you never heard of that website.

Trick growled at the screen and closed himself out of reddit. Rationally, he knew that Sickbird was probably right — there probably wasn't any money, and it wouldn't do him any good to try and collect it. And while he wanted the cash, his soul was worth more than a hundred grand, regardless of what some faceless Internet weirdo like Sickbird thought.

What he *really* thought was that the guy making the offer might be the Needle Man. Because who else would care that much? Nobody, except the kidnapper who was trying to get his kidnappee back. And May, obviously.

Something else Sickbird said was nagging at him: the princess's dad. He couldn't recall a single mention of a father anywhere in the webcomic, but then again, he hadn't read the whole thing straight through. He'd only read bits and pieces, mostly when he'd seen a friend link it around when a new page went up.

So what about the dad?

May said that Libby's father had moved back to Detroit or something, after his wife's and daughter's alleged deaths. Ten minutes traipsing through the brighter, more normal Internet spaces gave Trick a name and an address in Michigan.

But another five minutes gave him an old *Seattle Post-Intelligencer* link. And a heart attack:

MAN FOUND DEAD IN NORTHGATE DUMPSTER

Tuesday night a former Microsoft employee's body was found in a Dumpster behind the Northgate Mall.

IN TIME, THE RIGHT MOMENT ARRIVED.

WHAT'S THAT?

THE STORM MUST'VE KNOCKED THE POWER OUT. STAY PUT.

I'M SCARED.

POP

DON'T BE AFRAID. I'LL GET SOME CANDLES.

A FLASHLIGHT, MAYBE.

HEY, HAVE YOU SEEN THE FLASHLIGHT?

I CAN'T FIND IT.

OF COURSE YOU CAN'T, IDIOT.

THIS WAY. FOLLOW ME.

LAST FERRY DEPARTED
NEXT FERRY 6:00 AM

FOR THE SECOND TIME IN HER LIFE, PRINCESS X DISAPPEARED INTO THE WATER.

TEN

May heard her dad's key in the lock again, so she slammed her laptop shut.

She did it out of pure reflex, and then she felt stupid for it. Her dad already knew she was investigating Princess X, and it wasn't like the information she'd found so far was any big secret. Some of the conversations on the fan forums were ridiculous. People picked apart everything from the shade of red chosen for the princess's shoes to the numerology of the character names, trying to figure out if there was any mystical significance to any of it. And then you had the kids who were *so* into anime that everything had to be about ninjas, honor, and warrior culture.

May's dad called from the living room: "May? Are you home?"

"Yeah, I'm home," she shouted back. She checked to make sure her laptop was plugged in properly — it had turned out that Trick was right, and it really just needed a full recharge to work again — and then climbed down off her bed to say hello. Her knees were cramping up anyway.

She strolled into the living room, where her dad dropped a satchel onto the coffee table with a rustling thump. "You're home early," May said. "I thought your note said it would be a long day."

"It's after seven," he noted, cocking his head toward the clock on the wall.

"Oh. Then . . . you're home *late*."

"Turned out, my workday wasn't as long as I thought it'd be — so I made a stop on the way back. Are you hungry?"

"I'd eat some pizza, if anybody decided to order one. You know. Hypothetically."

"Anybody like me, right?" On the fridge was a magnet with the phone number and hours for a pizza joint not far away. Her dad plucked it off the door and dug his phone out of his pocket. "Any preference for toppings?"

"Nothing with eyeballs," she said.

"No anchovies. Got it."

"Or anything *else* with eyeballs. Don't get creative."

He grinned at her, dialed, and put in an order for something that would probably still be at least a little bit gross, because that was just how he rolled. She sat down in front of the TV and flipped around, but there was nothing good on, so she closed her eyes and leaned her head back against the wall. She thought maybe her dad would sit down beside her and change the channel from Comedy Central to CNN, but he didn't. He sat across from her in the recliner and turned down the volume to zero. May opened her eyes as he shoved his satchel across the coffee table.

"What's this?" she asked.

"It's for you. It's everything I could find at the library."

She sat forward, opened the satchel, and took out a little stack of paper. It was mostly photocopies, held together with paper clips and binder clippies. "It's all . . . about that night. The accident."

The one that wasn't an accident. The one that killed Mrs. Deaton.

"Yup. I pulled up a couple of weeks of material, since most of the reporting happened after the crash. I knew you'd be hunting around on the Internet, but those news sites don't archive stories forever. So I thought you might hit a dead end or two, and this would help. Look, see — here's one. It's dated the sixth, but it took them a few days to find the car, and then another day to raise it out of the water."

"I remember," she murmured, pulling the top few segments into her lap.

MOTHER AND DAUGHTER FEARED LOST IN BRIDGE ACCIDENT

DIVERS LOCATE CAR OF MISSING WOMAN

"And then a few more days before they found Libby."

"It wasn't Libby," she murmured again.

BODY OF MISSING MOTORIST IDENTIFIED

Her dad cleared his throat. "Well, it was a teenage girl. She was wearing Libby's clothes, and had Libby's student ID in her back pocket."

SEARCH CONTINUES FOR MISSING GIRL

"Is that how her dad identified her body? If she'd been in the ocean for a week . . ." She didn't finish the thought.

"Yeah. A week in the water. That's why they closed the casket, remember?"

She'd rather not.

BODY FOUND AT MARINA LIKELY THAT OF MISSING GIRL

She looked up from the papers. The headlines were making her cross-eyed. "Did they do a DNA test? I mean, surely they don't just bury people and assume that the tombstone and the body will just . . . magically match up."

"I doubt there was any formal test," he admitted. "They're pretty expensive, and no one else matching that description had gone missing or anything. Libby's ID sealed the deal, I guess. There was no reason to think it might be anybody else."

But the Ghost Mother's words were scrolling behind her eyes: *The Needle Man's kingdom is built on sand and the corpse of his own child, which he threw into the water.* So she said out loud, "It was his own daughter. She died, and he switched their bodies. He threw his own daughter into the Bay, and passed her off as Libby."

"You mean the Needle Man?"

She narrowed her eyes at him. "You've been reading *Princess X*?"

"The Internet is full of mysteries. Some are easier to solve than others."

"But they're *all* solvable," she insisted, gathering up the papers into her lap. "Every last one of them. Including this one. Hey, Dad?"

"Yeah?"

"Thanks."

"You're welcome," he said, a little awkwardly. "I just . . . you know. Felt bad, about how we didn't tell you. And now you know, so . . ."

"Yeah. Now I know."

"Maybe it'll help you figure out a few more clues if you read these along with the website. I don't know."

"It's worth a shot." She glanced down at her lap.

Anything was worth a shot.

A few minutes later, the pizza guy buzzed and they put the papers away. As it turned out, the only gross topping was roasted corn. Who puts roasted corn on anything? Much less on pizza? Her father was clearly deranged.

After they ate, she excused herself and went back into her bedroom, the stack of library photocopies under her arm. She opened up her laptop, which now had IAmPrincessX.com for a home page.

The screen flickered. The system booted back up, and the fairy tale began in earnest.

May read and read and read.

SILVERDALE

THE PRINCESS'S
KINGDOM LIES IN RUINS.

THE QUEEN IS DEAD.

THE KING IS EXILED.

AND THE PRINCESS WAS TAKEN AWAY.

TEMPORARILY.

Throughout the adventures that followed, Princess X and her mother always moved forward on their quest for the Four Keys: a gold mask, a red box, and a black mirror. The fourth key was the gray child — which made *Libby* the final puzzle piece, didn't it? Libby was the key who could vanquish the Needle Man, and free herself and her kingdom once and for all.

As for the other three keys . . . Well, May thought about the other three a lot as she went through the papers her dad had so kindly provided. There might be some kind of real-world versions of the keys — since Libby was a real-world version of the gray child. But what would they look like? A mask, a box, a mirror. Any of them could be just about anything, but surely Libby would give her hints, or clues. She just had to read everything closely, that's all.

As she pondered the possibilities and scrutinized all the information she had at hand, she learned that her dad was right about the dead-link thing. When she googled around, chasing more details of the Deaton family's case, she ran into a lot of 404-NOT FOUND nonsense, which seemed ridiculous when the case was only three years old. Some of the pages were cached, and she could look them up that way, but for the most part, she felt she was hunting in the wrong places. Somehow, she'd been handed all the clues . . . and she kept following them into dead ends. The deeper she went into the story, the more she felt like she was losing the thread of it. She was getting further away from the point.

But she still didn't have any doubts.

She *knew* Libby was alive, and that she was trying to draw May out to tell her something — ask her for a rescue or to set her free. She just felt miles away from understanding *how*. Light-years, even. Farther away than if Libby really was dead.

When Libby was dead, at least May knew where to find her.

CAPTAIN
OF THE GUARD

I FEAR THIS MIGHT NOT WORK OUT VERY WELL.

BUT THESE ARE THE MEN OF THE ROYAL GUARD. THEY WILL REMEMBER ME, AND THEY WILL HELP ME FIND THE KEYS.

BUT THINGS HAVE CHANGED, MY DEAR. YOU HAVE CHANGED. THEY HAVE CHANGED.

STOP RIGHT THERE!

BUT I AM PRINCESS X! I'VE ESCAPED THE NEEDLE MAN'S LAIR, AND I'VE COME HERE TO SEEK YOUR HELP.

PRINCESS X IS DEAD.

BUT THE NEEDLE MAN WARNED US THERE WOULD COME AN IMPOSTER — WEARING HER CLOTHES AND CARRYING HER SWORD.

I AM SORRY, BUT THE ROYAL GUARD WILL NOT HELP YOU. DON'T HATE THEM. IT'S NOT THEIR FAULT . . . NOT ENTIRELY.

THEN I WILL FIND ANOTHER WAY.

I WILL USE WHAT I AM GIVEN. I WILL FIND SOMEONE WHO KNOWS ME AND WILL HELP ME. I WILL GO AND FIND MY FATHER.

YOU HAVE ALWAYS BEEN GOOD AT FINDING OTHER WAYS. IT IS YOUR GREATEST STRENGTH.

May needed someone to talk to, so the next day, she threw caution to the wind, called Trick, and asked him to come down to her apartment. He already knew she lived in the building, and if his hacking skills were worth half of what he proclaimed them to be, he probably could've guessed her address anyway. For that matter, he could always just read the mailbox names downstairs. Sometimes the easiest answer was the analog one.

He knocked right on time, looking a little rumpled and kind of nervous. He looked past her shoulder and said, "Don't you live with your dad or something?"

"He's at work. Come on in."

"Does he care that I'm here? Alone with you? When he's not home?"

She frowned at him. "Why? Are you going to try something?"

"What? *No.*" Then he came to some decision, shrugged, and said, "You know what? It's fine. We can always just tell him I'm fixing your computer or whatever. Since I practically fixed your computer and all."

She held the door open and let him inside. "You can't fix it if it ain't broken. And there's no need to make anything up. He trusts me, pretty much."

"He does?"

"Well, it's like there's a halfway point," she tried to explain. "Right between him trusting me and not really caring what I do with my spare time. Either way, he's not going to shoot you if he finds you here."

"Very reassuring." Trick dropped himself onto the couch and tossed his bag onto the coffee table with a thump. Pretty much everyone tossed their stuff there, now that May thought about it. It was basically the lint trap for the entire apartment. She went to the kitchen to snag some sodas. As Trick made himself comfortable, he said, "You must not get into much trouble."

She leaned around the corner and said, "I'm not some boring Goody Two-shoes, if that's what you're implying. I'm just not into the stuff most parents find objectionable. Do you want a Coke or anything?"

"Sure. Hook me up."

They cracked the cans open, almost in perfect sync.

Trick asked, "So did you get any reading done last night, or what?"

She told him that, yes, she'd gone pretty far into the web series. "I also spent some time going through this stuff my dad found for me." She gestured toward the stack of papers she'd left out on the table.

"What are those?" he asked, leaning forward to pick them up.

"Police reports, news articles, that kind of thing, all about Mrs. Deaton's murder."

"Hmm . . ." He gazed pensively at the papers, flipping through them one after another. "You know, I remember this case. I remember seeing pictures of the girl on the news, and thinking she was pretty. This is wild," he said, more to the papers in his lap than to May. "I never would've put it together — this case and the website. It's not a perfect match, but there's enough for a good conspiracy theory."

"What do you mean, it's not a perfect match? There's the water, the mother killed with a gun, the girl —"

He cut her off. "Yeah, but there's no island and no kidnapping in reality . . . not so far as anyone else knows. Since the real-life stuff in the story is fairly short, people don't pay as much attention to that part. They're more interested in the fairy tale. Nobody has any reason to think the comics set in the real world are . . . well . . . real. Except for you, and now me. I think you've made me a convert."

"Good. Wait, why?"

"Because I found out what happened to Libby's dad, in real life."

"What are you talking about? Her dad went back to Detroit, I told you."

"Yeah, but that's not where he died. Did you know he was dead?"

She stared at him. "No . . . ?" she squeaked. She cleared her throat and tried again. "I didn't know him very well; he was just my friend's dad, you know? I haven't seen him since the funeral. But he's . . . he's dead? When? How? What happened?"

"Skip ahead to the Old King chapter in the comic. You get a story about how the princess calls him for help, but he never makes it. The Needle Man murders him and throws his body into a Pit of Infinity."

"Oh *God* . . . you mean . . ."

He reached into his messenger bag and whipped out an article he'd printed off the Internet. It was a *Seattle Post-Intelligencer* piece from about two years ago.

By the end of the article, May's throat was so dry that she couldn't even cough. "A Dumpster. Mr. Deaton was shot in the head, and left in a Dumpster. How did I not hear about this . . . ?" she asked herself more than Trick. She checked the date and realized it had happened in the fall, when she would have been living with her mother in Atlanta. "I guess it didn't make the national news."

"No reason it should have. People get murdered all the time, all over the place. Nobody could possibly report them all."

"You're really great at comforting people, you know that?"

"I do what I can." He tried to make it sound ironic, but it mostly made him sound like a jerk, which he apparently noticed. "I mean, I'm sorry. That's what I meant."

"And you said there's a bit about this, in the comic?"

"The Old King. You can read it later; it's a pretty good chapter. Or," he said quickly, "it's not *good*. Especially now that I know it was about a real thing, happening to a real guy. But it's interesting."

"I know what you meant. And I'll get to it, even if I have to read all night. I can't believe it. . . ."

Trick admitted, "I couldn't, either. I didn't really believe you, but this was kind of a nail in the coffin. Oh, crap, that was a bad way to put it."

"Maybe you should just stop talking."

But he couldn't, not yet. "I *would*, I would totally stop talking, but I can't — see, I think this guy . . . whoever the Needle Man is in real life . . . I think he's looking for her, same as we are. He's offered up a reward for anyone who can find her, and if he's the guy who killed her dad, then he's *hella*-dangerous."

"He killed Mrs. Deaton and kidnapped Libby. He's obviously hella-dangerous. And what do you mean, he's offered up a reward? Where? Show me!"

"I'm . . . uh . . . not sure I could find it again," he said, and never in her life had May been quite so certain that someone was lying. "But I'm sure it was him, and he's up to no good. If he was just some guy looking for a runaway daughter or something, he'd try to find her in all the usual, public ways. He wouldn't go sneaking around on the darknet. We've got to be careful with this," he concluded grimly. "We have to keep a low profile and make sure we don't catch this guy's attention."

She handed the printout back to him. "That's always been the plan. We solve who writes *Princess X*, one of the great mysteries of our time, *and* two murders and a kidnapping . . . and nobody sees us."

"There's no such thing as nobody seeing you on the Internet. Not really, no matter what anyone tells you. There's always some way to backtrack you."

"Now *you* sound like a nutjob conspiracy theorist."

Something about the look he flashed her said she'd touched a sore spot. He said, "I'm a realist. If *I'm* worried, *you* should be worried." He swilled his soda. "Give me your WiFi password, and while you read, I'll do some more digging on the net."

IT WASN'T YOUR FAULT.

BUT I CALLED FOR HIM. I ASKED HIM TO COME BACK AND SAVE ME. THE NEEDLE MAN WARNED ME . . . HE TOLD ME HE'D KILL ANYONE WHO TRIED TO HELP ME.

BUT I WANTED TO GO HOME.

AND YOU WILL, SOMEDAY

BUT NOT UNTIL WE'VE FOUND THE FOUR KEYS, SO WE MUST BEGIN OUR SEARCH ALONE. THE FIRST IS THE GOLD MASK.

BUT I DON'T KNOW WHERE TO LOOK. I CANNOT DO THIS ALONE. I NEED HELP, BUT I CAN'T ASK FOR IT.

YOU HAVE ME, ALWAYS. YOU HAVE YOUR GIFT FOR FINDING HIDDEN PATHS. YOU HAVE THE GHOSTS, THE WOLVES, AND THE PRINCE OF THE NIGHT CATS. AND BEST OF ALL, YOU HAVE THE JACKDAW — WHO KEEPS YOUR SECRETS, AND KEEPS YOU SAFE.

BUT I AM A DANGER TO THEM ALL.

AND THEY ARE A DANGER TO EVERYONE ELSE.

THERE IS AN ASKING POOL IN THE FOREST OF NOD. THE CAT PRINCE WILL PROTECT ME THERE.

I HOPE YOU'RE RIGHT. BUT NONE OF THEM CAN HELP ME FIND THE GOLD MASK — FOR THEY HAVE ALREADY TRIED AND FAILED.

I SEEK A GOLD MASK, SO I CAN FREE MYSELF AND MY KINGDOM FROM THE NEEDLE MAN. CAN YOU TELL ME WHERE TO FIND IT?

YES, BUT IT WILL NOT HELP YOU VANQUISH HIM. NOT BY ITSELF.

NO, NOT BY ITSELF. BUT IT IS THE FIRST PIECE OF THE PUZZLE, AND I MUST COLLECT IT.

THEN GO TO THE DARK CUP. YOU WILL FIND IT THERE, WITHIN THE EMPTY CHALICE. YOU MUST PULL IT FROM THE FIRE.

ELEVEN

"It's this right here. This bit . . ." May jabbed at the screen with her finger. She had been reading for two hours.

"What?" he asked eagerly, scooting to the edge of the seat.

"Here," she said, turning the screen around to show him. "Look what the puddle says: 'Go to the dark cup. You will find it there, within the empty chalice.'"

"So?"

"There used to be this coffeehouse down the hill called Black Tazza. Me and Libby spent a crap ton of time there back in the day."

"Yeah, I remember that place. It shut down a couple of years ago, then it reopened as something else."

"Stumptown bought it out. But *tazza*," she declared triumphantly, "means 'cup' in Italian. I know that because this barista kept trying to impress us with random bits of knowledge, even though we were *way* too young for him."

Trick got a big smile on his face, but it was tempered with a touch of confusion. "You think there's a real key? And it's hidden at Stumptown?"

"Bingo. The dark cup, the empty chalice . . . a coffee cup is kind of like a chalice, right?"

"Maybe, if you say so. But it's a stretch. A vague stretch."

"I know." She leaped up off the couch. "But maybe I'll figure it all out when I get there. So are you in, or out? We could both use a break."

He scrambled to his feet and retrieved his bag. "Okay, then. Let's ride."

They caught the number 12 bus and sat down between an old lady in a purple suit and a fat man in flip-flops. They could've walked the distance in twenty minutes, but May thought it was worth bumming a couple of quarters to spare themselves the hike.

Trick pulled the stop buzzer when they reached the right block . . . but once they were standing in front of it, it looked like the *wrong* block. Half of the buildings weren't there anymore, knocked down by the bulldozers parked atop the rubble. Everything that was left had been cordoned off.

"What happened?" May said. "I just walked by this place a few days ago! Everything was closed, but come *on!*"

"Development moves fast around here. Or demolition does, when condos are going up," Trick grumbled under his breath. "Look, they're leaving the old storefronts in place so they can call the building 'historic' and charge more for it. But see? Half of it is still standing. Maybe we got here in time."

She stared dubiously at the storefronts that remained — the Stumptown front among them. It'd been stripped bare, with only the shadows of the sign above the door, and the hours written in peeling paint on a window. She cocked a thumb at the big metal chain and padlock that secured the front entrance. "But it's all locked up. How are we supposed to get inside?"

He elbowed her in the ribs and smiled. "You're not some boring Goody Two-shoes, right? They've torn off the back half of the building. There's literally no *way* they could've secured it all the way around."

"Do you do a lot of trespassing?" she asked, trying to sound casual and not concerned. She might feel better if he was experienced at this sort of thing.

"Mostly the digital kind, but this kind too. Once in a while," he added, leading her around the far side of the block.

"Have you ever been caught?"

"Once or twice."

"And did they just . . . do they arrest you, or let you go, or what?"

"They let me go as soon as my mom posted bail," he said brightly. "But that's not going to happen to *us*. We're going to be careful."

"You weren't careful last time?"

"Not careful enough." He scanned the boundaries of the cordoned-off zone. "But this will be way easier than getting out of a mall after dark. We'll be done and gone in a few minutes, and no one will know the difference."

Finding out that he'd done this before didn't make her feel any better after all.

The whole block was roped off with a temporary fence — the orange plastic kind that looks like a very long net. It was wrapped around matching orange barrels, and adorned with a dozen signs, all of which suggested they find something less controversial to do with their time. Trick ignored them and went to one corner of the plastic fence. He lifted it up like the hem of a lady's skirt. "See? No big deal. Go on in."

"Me first?"

"I'm right behind you."

She took him at his word and crawled under the netting. As she waited for him to follow, she looked up and found a hundred vantage points where anyone could be watching them from a window. It was too easy for someone to get nosy and call 911 to report a couple of kids snooping around a construction site.

Trick went ahead of her over the rubble, sliding here and there, catching himself on some of the bigger chunks of building detritus. He used long, protruding sticks of rebar to keep his balance. May climbed up after him. It looked easy from below, like crossing a playground full of gravel, but it was more like rock climbing without any gear.

"Once we get inside," Trick said, then paused to scoot forward again, "no one will be able to see us."

"Unless there are security cameras."

He looked over his shoulder, either to check that she was still coming or to make sure she saw the grumpy frown he flashed her way. "Why would you say a thing like that? Can't you just enjoy a little adventure?"

"Yeah, *but* . . ." She pointed up at the street corner, where some of the demolition equipment was parked. What looked like a big camera was mounted on a pole beside it, aimed right into the postapocalyptic courtyard they were doing their best to cross.

"Oh," he said. "They're probably just for show. Most places don't even turn those things on. But hurry up, just in case."

"Just in case," she muttered behind him, sliding down a slab of cement the size of a dinner table.

Trick was almost at the rear of the storefront block, or what was left of it. It looked like it'd been sheared in two, exposing the interiors in a way that was very naked and kind of sad. Dangling pipes and bathroom tiles jutted into the open air, and fluffy strips of insulation flapped in the damp, mildew-smelling breeze. He climbed up into one of the gaping holes and held out a hand. "Come on. You've got it. And see? We don't have to break in. Everything's already broken."

She took his hand and let him pull her up, even though the drop-off was only a couple of feet; and soon she was standing beside him, next to a brick wall that ended abruptly in a ragged edge. "Which store did this used to be?" she asked.

"The pizza place, I think."

As he said it, she noticed the remains of the counter shoved against one wall, where part of a menu was left on a chalkboard. The word *pepperoni* jumped out at her. "Yeah, this was definitely the pizza place."

Trick looked a little lost. His eyes swept back and forth in the gloomy, unfamiliar space. "Where do we go from here?"

"To the right," she said firmly. "You see this corridor that ran through the middle, connecting all the stores in this building? That's where the only bathroom was; all the businesses shared it. Hey, I can't see anything back there. You got a light? The flashlight app on my phone is kind of crappy."

"I've got a little light."

"That's fine."

"It's *really* little," he warned her. "Key chain little. We should've brought something bigger."

"I didn't know they were tearing the place down. Did you?"

He shook his head. "No. But I still feel unprepared." He pushed a button, and she heard a tiny click as the light came on.

He wasn't kidding about the light being small — it was just barely better than a phone would be. She looked around, and realized they'd found the pizza parlor's seating area. Framed travel brochures and broken fixtures hung crookedly, and built-in booths covered in dust lined the narrow space. "Um . . . now we should go *this* way."

"You don't sound sure."

"I'm not. But it's either *this* way, or *that* way —" She gestured toward the other direction. "There's nowhere else to go, except back into the yard." Emboldened by her own ironclad logic, she took his key chain light away from him.

"Hey!"

"Am I leading the way or not?"

The hallway was as tall as any normal hallway, but they crouched along it all the same, listening hard for any sign that they weren't alone. If it was this easy for May and Trick to get inside, there was no telling who else had gotten the bright idea to poke around the ruins, and the tiny light gave off just enough glow to make everything look really, really creepy. May went slow enough that Trick stayed pretty close, practically hugging her, and under different circumstances she might've objected to feeling his breath on her shoulder, or the constant knocking of his elbows and knees against her back and legs. But for the moment, she was glad to have him with her.

They came to a big door painted red. It had a red-and-white exit sign above it.

She nodded vigorously. "This is it. This is the way. There's a hallway back here." She leaned against the horizontal door lever, and the fastener clicked. The door swung outward.

"Cool," he declared. "I was afraid it'd be locked."

"Me too."

They both stalled there at the edge. If it was dark inside the pizza place, it was even darker in the hallway beyond it. The key chain light felt very small, and the building felt very big, despite being cut in half and partly torn down. There was still plenty left to get lost in.

"Which way?" he asked, nudging her with the back of his hand.

She tried to think. "If we're standing in the back of the pizza joint, then Black Tazza was to the right. So let's go right, and see what we find," she said. But she didn't move. They were talking just to hear themselves, afraid of the dark like little kids.

"Ladies first."

"Again?"

"All right, then give me back the light and *I'll* go first."

"No," she said. "I'm going, I'm going."

"Make up your mind."

So she went. Small steps, slowly performed, down the pitch-black hall that felt like a tunnel ready to collapse any second. Trick stayed even closer now, and his breathing was quick behind her. They didn't talk anymore, and the only sounds were the scrape of their feet on the dirty floors, kicking at dusty rubble and tripping over broken tiles. Somewhere off in the distance, a slow drip of water splashed into a puddle.

To their left, May saw a door. "That's the bathroom Black Tazza used. We're on the right track."

She kept telling herself that she and Trick weren't *really* underground, after all. They were only locked inside a place so decrepit that it'd meet a wrecking ball within a week. This was the most dangerous or ridiculous thing she'd ever done. And what if she was wrong about all the keys being real? This could all be for nothing, except a bunch of scrapes, bruises, and maybe a fresh tetanus shot.

"Over here. This door, this is it." She reached for the knob. It stuck fast and wouldn't budge.

"Locked?" Trick asked.

"Yeah, this one's locked."

"Okay, don't panic."

"Nobody's panicking," she assured him.

"Good. Because I brought this." He took out a pocketknife and extended the blade.

She wasn't so sure of that. "You can pick a lock with a pocketknife?"

"Probably. And it's not just a pocketknife, it's a multitool."

But "probably" meant "no." The lock refused to be picked, no matter which slim blade Trick chose to stab it with.

"Forget it." May turned away from him and the door. "I have a better idea. Stay here for a second."

"Alone? In the dark?"

"I'm not going very far. I saw something useful over here."

There on the ground: a large chunk of cinder block, too large to carry with one hand. She put the flashlight in her mouth, picked up the block, and tucked it against her ribs to carry it back to the door.

"Take the light," she said, her words distorted as she moved her lips around it.

Gingerly, he retrieved it with two fingers. Then he wiped her spit on his pants.

"Now shine it on the door, okay?"

With no small degree of effort, she raised the cinder block above her shoulders and brought it down on the knob. She hit it again, and a third time, and on the fourth blow it broke off, rattling down to the floor and rolling away in the dark. She bashed the door a final time, and the lock mechanism fell out of the hole, falling to the old ceramic floor with a clatter.

May dropped the cinder block. She put her weight against the door and it scraped open, leaving a rainbow arc swept clean on the dusty floor.

"And here I thought you didn't want to break and enter," Trick said.

"Dude, shut up."

On the other side of the broken door, light from the windows filtered in, even though they were mostly covered with butcher's paper and city permit signs. Trick put the key chain light away. They could see the bar at the window with two stools left behind, and places where the ceiling tiles had fallen inward and stray bits of wire dangled down, trailing like jungle vines in primary colors. May let out a small laugh.

"What's so funny?"

"It's almost cleaner now than when it was Black Tazza."

"So . . . this is the place?" He kicked at a bit of rubble on the floor. "What a dump."

"Yeah. Keep your eyes open for something like . . . something like fire, I guess. Or something hot. Something related to fire, somehow . . . ?"

"You still have no idea, do you?"

"Nope. But Princess X found a gold mask in the fire, and there's some kind of empty chalice at work."

They split up, but they didn't get very far apart. The place wasn't that big, and they were always within eyesight of each other . . . on purpose, whether or not they would've admitted it. May checked the walls, in case any of the graffiti had any clues to offer; then she checked under the counters, inside the cabinets, and underneath the bench seats, which opened up if you knew where to lift them. She found an unopened pack of coffee filters, pieces of several broken mugs, and a phone book from 2009.

"Any luck?" she called over to Trick, who was standing on tiptoes, combing the storage shelves.

"A moldy sleeve of to-go cups. A stack of plastic ashtrays. Three cracked saucers, a bunch of sweetener packets, and more spiders than you really want to hear about."

When they had exhausted all possible chalices, they stood there in silence. Finally, May threw her hands up and said, "I guess I was wrong about this place. But it was worth a shot, wasn't it?"

"Totally worth a shot, I agree. And hey, it's a good thing we tried *now*. Imagine if you'd gotten the idea after the place was torn down. You'd be kicking yourself for the rest of your life."

She laughed nervously. "That's true. Oh, well. Get your dinky little flashlight ready. Let's get out of here before we get caught."

Trick obliged, and they exited the way they'd come in. The coffee-house door closed behind them, with the freshly empty doorknob hole now spilling a feeble column of light. It didn't help much, or for very long. Once again they shuffled forward, always on the alert for the sound of construction equipment or crazy hobos.

When they reached the bathroom door again, May hesitated. She put her hand on Trick's arm, and the light he held bobbed up and down, throwing weird shadows on his face. "Wait a minute. Let's check the bathroom before we go."

"All right. But make it quick. This place is creepy as hell."

"It's not creepy." She wrestled with the latch. "Not exactly. It's not like an old hospital, or a hotel, or someplace where a bunch of people have died." The bathroom door squeaked open, swinging outward when she gave it a yank. "Give me the light again, would you?"

"No. I like holding it. Just tell me where you want me to shine it."

"Fine, but it's kind of cramped in here for two people."

"Yuck."

She couldn't argue with him there. The small room gobbled up all the key chain light and reflected some of it back at them — because a big, cracked mirror filled most of one wall. They looked like something out of a found-footage horror flick; their heads and hands were dirty, and their eyes were huge, their pupils way too big. They stared into the glass as if they half expected something to appear behind them, and it was scarier to look away than to just keep looking.

No monsters, no Bloody Mary. Nothing but . . .

"Hey . . ." she said, pointing to a spot in the mirror. "Turn around."

They turned around together to face the toilet. Trick aimed the key chain at the uncovered bowl like a spotlight, revealing long streaks of rust inside, but nothing else. Then May nudged his hand up, just a little. The beam focused on the tank, and then on a spot above it, settling upon a big flash of graffiti.

"Is that . . . a crown? A hat or something?" he asked.

"No," May said, stepping closer. Elegant tendrils of red and yellow stretched along the wall, with light wisps of smoke curling at the top. "Check it out, Trick. It's *fire*."

"Fire coming out of a toilet tank? What were they serving in that pizza place?" he joked weakly.

"No, look at this — this artwork is *good*. Not like crappy street art. Like a real artist did it."

"You think it was your friend?"

May took a deep breath and lifted the lid off the tank. "I don't know. Bring the light over. There's something in here." She put all thoughts of spiders and toilet water out of her mind, reached inside, and withdrew a gallon-size ziplock bag, its exterior swaddled in duct tape.

"Oh, wow," she said, shaking the water off, and then dusting the bag on her jeans. It was lumpy, and almost weightless. "Your pocketknife," she gestured wildly. "Give it here."

He forked it over (with only a small complaint about its being a "multitool, dammit"), and she sat on the edge of the toilet seat, even though it was inexcusably gross. Carefully, she took one of the little blades and ran it along the outermost seam, making sure she didn't damage anything inside. Once she'd cut a good long slit in the plastic, she shoved her hand through it and felt around.

"Come on, show me," he begged. "What *is* it?"

She unwound a strip of opaque plastic sheeting to reveal a mask, just like the webcomic suggested. But it wasn't a masquerade piece, or a rubber Halloween jobbie.

Trick frowned. "Is that . . . a surgical mask?"

May turned it over and saw something drawn inside it — a pair of eyes. On the left eye was written, in firm, bold print: 58921. On the right: 44228. "Looks like it. What was the riddle? A gold mask with secrets in its eyes? Well, it's yellow, anyway. Close enough, right?"

He nodded anxiously and peered down at the scrap of fabric. "What do those numbers mean? Do you recognize them?"

"I don't know. I've never seen them before."

They stared at it in silence while May racked her brain, trying to figure out what it meant. "I guess it *might* be a phone number . . . ? It's got enough digits. 589 . . . what's that area code?"

"I don't know." Trick pulled out his phone and dialed, leaving it on speakerphone and holding it out between them. They hovered over the glow of the smartphone's screen, on pins and needles until the classic chime of *"Doo bee doop — We're sorry, but this number is no longer in service"* left them both disappointed. He said, "Well, it doesn't really look like a phone number anyway. Or a Social Security number, either," he noted.

"Maybe a patient ID," she suggested. "Since it's written on a hospital mask and all."

He brightened. "That's a really good idea. We can use that as a starting point. Let's head back home and do some research."

May stood up and stuffed the mask and all its packaging into her messenger bag. "As far as research goes, we're at the mercy of your elite hacker skills."

"That's what you pay me for. If you *do* ever pay me."

"You'll get your six-fifty one of these days."

They found their way outside quickly, and it was with great relief that they stepped into the daylight and rubble. Not into the sun, exactly, because the sky had gone all overcast while they were in there; but they were in the open again, and they could breathe and see again, without the feeble help of that stupid key chain light.

May wiped her cheek with her sleeve, and left a streak of dust. Even if she'd seen it, she wouldn't have cared. "So — hey! I was right! The keys are real!"

"You were right! About . . . something!"

She smacked him on the shoulder, but they were both grinning like idiots. "Come on, let's get home. We can catch the bus on the next street over."

They vibrated with excitement the whole ride back up the hill. They tried to keep quiet and not twitch too much, but as soon as they threw themselves off the bus and onto the sidewalk, Trick jumped up in the air. "I still can't believe it!" he said. "We actually solved one of the riddles!"

"Well, *I* solved one of the riddles — and I told you it was Libby!"

"Yeah, yeah — you told me, I know. From here on out, I'll just assume you're a hundred percent right at all times."

"Actually, I'd love that. It's a shame you're probably lying."

"*Lying*'s such an ugly word. Let's say I'm exaggerating. Come on, we're almost home. Once I get back to my computer, I can run those numbers!"

TWELVE

Trick's place was actually his mom's place — or his mom and her boy-friend's, as he noted sourly. Neither of them was around. Trick told May to help herself to the fridge, so she did, and she was delighted to find Orange Crush. (Who drinks Orange Crush anymore? May, when she could get her hands on it, that's who.)

She guessed which room was Trick's on the first try, and sat down on the edge of his bed. She crossed her legs under herself and watched as he booted up a system that looked like a cross between a NASA computer and the world's biggest video game console. Dual monitors were lined up neatly beside a black-and-gray CPU tower, with a couple of external hard drives hooked up here and there, plus what looked like a network drive on the top shelf of the computer desk. Except for the Grumpy Cat sticker on the back of his chair, the whole setup said that *this* was a guy who took his computer time pretty dang seriously.

May watched as he adjusted things, pulled up menus, and opened windows into panels that looked like numbers on a black background to her. Without turning around, he said, "Let's start with the obvious, simple stuff. Read off those numbers."

She pulled the mask out of her bag and smoothed it out, then read the digits aloud. He entered them into a Google search field and called up a long string of links that she couldn't read from where she was sitting. "What's all that?"

He scrolled and scrolled, so fast that she couldn't believe he was actually reading it all. "The string is a partial match to a bunch of ISPs, but that doesn't mean anything. I don't see anything promising here. If you're right" — he turned around, propping his arm up on the back of the chair — "if it's a patient ID number of some kind, that wouldn't necessarily be public. I might have to poke around in some hospital databases."

"Is that legal?"

He gave a short little laugh. "No, but it can be done. Of course, it'd go quicker if we had any idea which hospital we were trying to hack."

"Start with Seattle hospitals. Libby lived here, so maybe the Needle Man did too. Hey, here's a thought: The webcomic said he had a daughter who died. Maybe this is *her* number, from when she was a patient."

Trick snapped his fingers at her. "Good thinking! We might be able to tie the Needle Man to a real person without going through any of the . . . um, 'back channels.' So let's start with what we already know." Beside his keyboard was a notebook. He grabbed a pen and started scrawling on it. "We know we're looking for a man old enough to be your dad, so let's say he's probably in his late thirties, at the youngest."

"A guy in his late thirties with a dead daughter."

"A daughter who would've died right around the time Libby did," he added, then jotted down the month and year of Libby's disappearance. "It'd have to be really close; otherwise he couldn't have used her body as a stand-in. And that's what the website says happened."

"Good point," she agreed. "This is good, we're getting somewhere."

"This guy could be from anyplace. He might not even be American — he could be Canadian just as easy. We need to narrow it down even further."

"Libby was biracial: half Japanese, half white. His daughter probably was too."

"Then this guy might be Asian."

She shook her head. "No, he doesn't look Asian. Not in the comic."

"Oh yeah, you're right. So we're talking about a white guy. And his daughter was sick. . . ." As they talked, he merrily typed away, his fingers working independently from his mouth. May hoped his brain was tuned in to the typing, not the yapping. "Something life-threatening, obviously. I mean, since she died from it. Something like cancer . . . or . . . I don't know, what else do people get sick and die from?"

"Infections? Bird flu?"

"Maybe, but I'm liking cancer. The Needle Man went looking for a match, right? A match for his daughter? It could be bone marrow."

"Or blood, or organs. Maybe she needed a kidney transplant. I knew a guy who had one of those. He had a big scar. Looked like he'd been bitten by a shark," she added.

"Okay, I'll add it to the list of maybes. But I'm still liking cancer."

"Nobody likes cancer," she said.

"You know what I mean."

While Trick worked, May scanned the bookshelves over his bed. They were full of comic books and magazines, with a few action figures to break up the reading material. She recognized Gordon Freeman from *Half-Life 2*, a Little Sister from *BioShock*, Drake from *Uncharted*, and a couple of *Halo* Spartans alongside some *Dragon Age* figures. Idly, she asked him, "Aren't you getting a little old for toys?"

"Aren't you getting a little old for princess fairy tales?" he retorted. "Help yourself to some reading. This might take a while."

"Should I order a pizza?"

"Yes. No. Maybe. Not yet," he decided. "Give me an hour. Data mining always makes me hungry."

She ended up giving him longer than an hour because she got wrapped up in his old *Transmetropolitan* trades. But before she could finish Spider Jerusalem's last foul-mouthed adventure, Trick sat up straight, adjusted one of his monitors, and enlarged a column of numbers. Then he barked, "Hey!"

May leaped up off the bed and came to stand behind him. "What have you got?"

"Seattle Children's Hospital. Since we're talking about sick kids and all, I started in pediatrics."

"Well played, dude. What'd you find?"

He pointed at the address window. He'd opened a PDF named XrbrClinicalTrials09. "You see this?"

"Clinical trials. Drug trials?"

"Yeah, for an experimental cancer drug called Xerberox. This is the patient manifest, but for privacy reasons, all the patients are identified by their case numbers — not their names."

"And you found the number from the mask?" It was almost too much to hope.

He slouched down in the chair, backing away from the keyboard but leaving his hand on the mouse. "I *did* find the number, yes. It's . . . Okay, to be honest, on second thought, this is not as helpful as I hoped it would be."

"Why not?"

With his left hand, he waved at the screen as if she should *totally* be able to see the problem for herself. She had no idea what she was staring at. It looked like a calculus test.

"Not only are we missing a name for this patient, we don't have any identifying characteristics, either," he said. "Not so much as a state of residence, or a gender, for that matter."

May wasn't ready to give up. "It's the first princess. It *has* to be, and now we know she was here in Seattle. We knew she was sick, and now we know it was cancer — just like you guessed. *And* now we know that, yes, for sure, the number on the mask was a medical case file. Why can't you just look up the case number at the hospital?"

"I tried that already."

"You did?"

"It was my first thought." He turned to look up at her.

"But you couldn't get inside?" she said, bringing her attention back to the important stuff.

He snorted. "Of *course* I got inside. The system's tight, but it's not Fort Knox. The problem is, the hospital clears out the records of deceased patients every three years. I assume they archive the stuff someplace, maybe at a storage facility somewhere; but it's probably in hard copy, in a box in the basement. Or something like that."

"Then we go find the basement. We start opening boxes."

"And go to jail. Go directly to jail. Do not pass GO. Do not collect two hundred dollars."

"Do you have any *better* ideas?" she asked, already wondering where she'd get a lock-pick kit and what the security system was like in a hospital basement.

"Give me a minute. Or two. Maybe five minutes." He looked up at her again. "There are a few more places I can check. Let's order that pizza." He gave the leftmost monitor another longing look, as if willing it to tell him something new and useful.

Then, to May's utter surprise, it *did*.

He wrinkled his brow and said, "Hey, that's weird." He sat forward, peering intently at the top of the window — at the address URL.

"What's weird?"

"The PDF isn't hosted on the hospital servers. It's on some private host, though the hospital is dialed into it. Hmm." He cut and pasted the address onto a Word document he was using for notes. "I'll look into that later. First, pizza."

"And then?"

"And then you go home and finish reading the webcomic. Or keep reading, anyway. I won't be able to do any really good digging until tonight, when the freaks come out."

May thought about staying for pizza, now that she knew Trick a little better. She liked his willingness to get into trouble, his blatant disregard for other people's privacy, and his businesslike approach to lawbreaking. But her dad would be home soonish, and she wanted some alone time with the mask, the message, and the website.

So instead, she told Trick good night and went back to her own place, to do some reading in private.

115

May sat propped up in her bed. She held the surgical mask in her hands and turned it over and over again, hunting for any small detail she might've missed. She didn't see anything new. Just a cheap, disposable mask made of cotton. It was that dull yellow color you see in hospitals and basically no place else, with four white ties that dangle down so you can fasten it behind your head.

And the handwriting on the back, written inside the oval shapes that passed for eyes. Was it Libby's handwriting? May struggled to remember what her script had looked like, concentrating hard to recall any note passed in class, any message left in the locker they shared. She recalled Libby's chicken-scratch penmanship well enough, but these numbers were printed in a big, blocky style that could've come from anyone. Maybe Libby didn't write them; maybe somebody did it for her. May wanted to believe she was holding an object that the real, still-alive Libby had touched, but she couldn't swear to it, and it annoyed her.

Aggravated with herself, and maybe with Princess X and Libby too, a little bit, she tossed the mask across the room. It hit her bedroom door and slid down to the carpet, where it lay crumpled in a wadded heap.

"Forget it," she said to herself. She reached for her bedside lamp to turn it off, but then she stopped, startled. Because the phone was ringing.

Not her cell phone, not her dad's cell phone. The landline, which she'd almost never heard before. She changed her mind about the super-early bedtime and rolled out of the covers, more curious than anything else. She tucked her feet into a pair of slippers shaped like fluffy white chickens and opened the door. By then the phone had stopped ringing. Her dad had answered it.

"Hello? Hello?"

He said that a few more times, then shrugged and hung up.

"Who was that?" she asked.

"Wrong number, I guess." He went back to the couch. "Are you turning in for the night already? It's only ten o'clock."

"I'm tired," she said.

"Big adventures today?"

She lied, "Nah. Just went and got coffee."

"With that computer kid?" May had told him about Trick the day before.

"Yeah. He's all right. He's someone to talk to while you're not home, anyway."

He halfway grinned. "You hardly talk to me when I'm here."

"I'm talking to you right now."

"Not about anything important."

"Trick's . . . Okay, you're right. Trick *isn't* important," she conceded, even though she knew it wasn't true as soon as she said it. At the moment, he was basically her only friend in the whole state. Except for Libby, maybe. She leaned against the door frame. "But Princess X is important, and you must be tired of hearing about *that*."

She spotted the mask lying by the door and used her toe to nudge it back farther into her room.

"It's interesting. One hell of a hobby you've got yourself."

"Proving that someone's alive, and maybe kidnapped, and maybe in danger? It's not a *hobby*, Dad."

"My apologies," he said, seriously enough that she was almost afraid he was making fun of her. "I didn't mean it like that. I should've called it a project or something. Poor word choice on my part. Please forgive me."

"Whatever," she said with a sigh, and let go of the doorjamb. She turned around to head for bed, but he called her name and she stopped.

"May — did you . . . did you learn anything useful from the library copies?"

She didn't want to be a jerk, not about the one thoughtful thing he'd done so far that summer. So she said, "Yes and no. I'm still going through it. It's a lot to read, and you know me. I'm slow."

"Okay. Well. I hope it's helpful."

"I'm sure it will be. Good night, Dad."

"Good night."

So she went to bed, and she wasn't mad.

She was almost asleep when the landline rang again, that ordinary electronic ringing, like out of some vintage TV show. She heard her father's voice saying, "Hello? . . . Hello? . . . Hello? Who is this?" He gave up, and hung up.

And then May was awake again, whether she liked it or not — so she thought she might as well get some reading done.

IT WAS THE WIZARD WHO LIVES BEHIND THE MOUNTAINS. HE SOLD ME THE CANDY-APPLE POTION FOR MY MOUTH, AND THEN HE WAS GONE.

YOU MUST ASK THE MERMAIDS IF YOU WISH TO FIND HIM AND VANQUISH THE NEEDLE MAN.

WHERE CAN I FIND THESE MERMAIDS?

THEY SWIM AND DIVE DOWN BY THE BRIDGES. THE DOVE CAN SHOW YOU THE WAY.

BUT THIS IS NOT A DOVE — THIS IS MY FRIEND THE JACKDAW.

NO, FOR A JACKDAW MUST BE AS BLACK AS NIGHT. YOUR FRIEND IS SOME OTHER BIRD.

A JACKDAW SHOULD APPEAR HOWEVER HE WISHES. AND THIS ONE WISHES TO HELP ME.

May smacked the laptop shut and reached for her phone. It was late by usual-people standards, but not very late according to Trick Standard Time — it wasn't even midnight yet. She pulled up their last phone interaction and called him back, muttering, "Come on, come on, come on," under her breath when it rang unanswered.

She wondered if he'd put her name into his phone. Surely by now, right? If it turned out that he was looking at his phone, seeing her name, and not picking up . . . she was going to smack him senseless. But maybe he'd turned the ringer off, or maybe the phone was dead. He might've even been talking to someone else, or in the shower, or some-place else where he wouldn't hear it.

So she tried again a few minutes later, to the same result. This time, she left a message. She left it quietly, because her dad was already asleep in the next room, but she left it *insistently*: "Dude, I think I've solved the next riddle! Meet me tomorrow morning for breakfast. Seriously. Breakfast. If your butt isn't out of bed by ten o'clock, I'm coming up there with a Taser and a pot of coffee."

THIRTEEN

Trick didn't hear the phone ring when May called, but even if he had, he might've ignored it. He had bigger problems than demanding downstairs neighbors with mysteries.

His machine had been compromised.

He knew it as soon as he logged on and let everything load up — something about the very slight, almost imperceptible difference in load time. And then, when he ran a system check, there it was: spyware. Someone had given him a nasty case of it.

He spent an hour or two desperately trying to clean it off, kick it off, or otherwise evict it, to no avail. It was hanging around, at least until he could figure out what it was and how to take it apart. It might take some research. Finally, he tried one of his favorite last-ditch scrubbers and rebooted his machine.

When he logged back on, a message was waiting for him on Gchat, even though he was supposed to be "invisible" and he wasn't supposed to get messages from unapproved parties. Gchat was really starting to drive him crazy.

BLACKBIRDWHITE: You there, Trick?

ZHATTRICKZ: Sickbird, I assume? Are you the one who trashed my machine?

BLACKBIRDWHITE: It's not trashed, it's just infected. Someone was curious about your data mining and followed you home. And no, that wasn't me — but it's easy enough to piggyback.

ZHATTRICKZ: You're a jerk.

BLACKBIRDWHITE: I'm giving you a warning, idiot. You need to be more careful, if you haven't blown it already, I don't know. You poked at something a very bad man was hosting, and now he's stuck you with a trolljan for your trouble. He's trying to figure out if it was an innocent trespass or if you're onto something.

ZHATTRICKZ: A trolljan? Are you a bad typist, or is that what this little script is called? Can you help me clear off my machine?

BLACKBIRDWHITE: Nah, I like being able to keep an eye on you, and the little script doesn't notice me watching over its shoulder. You've got another test or two to pass before you get any closer. I want to see how it goes.

The green dot beside BLACKBIRDWHITE went dark. Trick seethed, but the guy was gone. And if *trolljan* was a clue, or a test, or whatever . . . it wasn't a very good one.

Was it?

Maybe he should call May. On second thought, it was midnight, and she'd probably kill him if he tried it. A text ought to be safe, though.

Now, where the hell was his phone?

FOURTEEN

Trick was grumpy when he and May met for brunch the next morning, but he *did* come to brunch, and that was something. Nonetheless, he was in one righteously foul mood, May thought — not strictly because she had dragged him out of bed but also because someone, somewhere, had done something to his computer.

"I don't like it," he declared, waving a forkful of crepe at her face. "One minute my system is pristine, and the next I'm getting spyware out the ying-yang."

"What exactly *is* a ying-yang?" she said.

"Cute. Very cute. But you know what's not cute? *Spyware.* Really good spyware is *especially* not cute. It gets in your system, gums it up, and reports back to whoever programmed it."

"So uninstall it already. You're the IT guy."

"I tried! I'm still trying," he qualified. "I'm running a new scrubber on it now — it might be done by the time we finish up here and get back to the apartment. The whole thing is weird, and I know it has something to do with Princess X."

"Keep your voice down!" she said.

"My voice *is* down. Just like my system."

"Your system's not down, it's just . . . watching you. From a remote location, with dubious intent."

He got a little glint in his eye. "It *could* be the Needle Man, you know."

"You're just saying that because you think it might interest me," May said. "Spyware does not interest me. Try again."

"No, I'm serious." He wiped his mouth with his napkin, and assumed his Serious Conspiracy Theorist expression of earnest concern. "I first noticed the program right after you left yesterday — after we'd discovered the PDF of those clinical trials. You know how I said it wasn't hosted on hospital servers? Well, get this: The IP tracks back to Bainbridge Island, and it looks like the server there hosts a whole bunch of old hospital records. It's basically a digital version of the hospital basement, like I was talking about."

"Do hospitals do that? Offload their old records?"

"Lots of companies do," he assured her. "Law firms, hospitals, schools, publishers, you name it. Sometimes they want to keep old records for legal reasons or whatever, but they don't want to let the out-of-date stuff take up space on their own equipment — and there are too many security concerns with the cloud for some corporations to take a chance on it. No" — he tapped his fork on the edge of his plate — "I think this is a private server farm. And whoever's hosting it likes to keep an eye on the traffic."

"A server farm on Bainbridge? That's . . . not so far away."

"And it's an *island*. Princess X escaped from an island."

She liked where this was headed, but she wasn't quite ready to go there just yet. "The world is full of islands. Puget Sound is full of islands, for that matter. Look, it's *my* job to jump to conclusions, not yours."

"Take my hand. Jump with me."

She shook her head. "You think the Needle Man has been managing a server farm for years, archiving the records of his own daughter's medical history?"

"Not just *her* medical history: the whole report from the clinical trial and other drug trials too. It could be a coincidence, but I bet it's not. The Needle Man is a geek at least, and maybe even a hacker; it makes sense that he'd work in technology, like web hosting or server farming. They're the kind of jobs you can do from home, in isolation. All you need is something like a T1 Internet connection and you can manage your whole life right from your computer."

"It's still a big leap."

"But the host — whoever it was — attached a Trojan horse to the PDF so he could see if I was . . . You know, just an innocent trespasser who clicked the wrong link, or somebody who's curious about his dead daughter."

"Because that might mean someone made the connection between his dead daughter and my not-dead friend?" It was a reach, but she could see the pieces trying to fit together. They bounced against each other in her brain, struggling to form some bigger picture.

"Now you're thinking like I'm thinking!"

"How nerve-racking."

"But you see where I'm coming from, right? Maybe there were questions about his daughter's burial or cremation, or whatever — since we figure he probably tossed her into the Bay and let the cops believe it was Libby. There could be a million reasons he's been touchy about the information. . . . We don't even know what we don't know."

"That's the truest thing you've said so far."

"Yeah, well, *this* is even truer: This guy is watching me, through my computer. Now that we've found the PDF, he knows we're onto him."

"We aren't *really* onto squat."

"Oh, come on — you read it yourself in the comic: The Needle Man told the princess he'd kill her and everyone she cared about if she tried to leave him. We know her father turned up dead a couple of years ago, and we know he's been trying to draw people in with that reward, so we're not alone in looking for her. That PDF," he said under his breath, like he was still kicking himself. "That PDF was practically booby-trapped, and I walked right into it."

"Even if you're right, all that means is . . . is . . ." She paused. "I guess it means we have to be careful and move fast. But we were doing that already."

He wasn't listening. May could see it in the way he stared at his mostly empty plate, rearranging the crumbs and syrup with his eyes. He pulled out a credit card and threw it on the table. "Here, I'll get this one. Next one's on you."

May thought it must be nice to be able to eat out without looking at the bill or doing any math. He definitely didn't need her six-fifty.

"So now what?" he asked her, once the waitress had taken the card. "What's the big emergency that brings us together before noon?"

Oh yeah. She hadn't actually told him why she'd hauled him out of bed at such an ungodly hour. And by "ungodly hour" she meant "ten thirty."

"We're going to Fremont, because I've solved another riddle," she proclaimed.

He dipped a skeptical eyebrow. "What's in Fremont?"

"The troll."

He rolled his eyes. "Seriously?"

"What? There's a troll in the comic! And yes, I know it's obvious — I'm mostly joking. We're not going to visit the troll; we're going to follow the troll's instructions and find the mermaids instead." She picked up her messenger bag and her blue corduroy jacket.

"Mermaids? You think there are mermaids in Fremont?"

"I know it for a fact," she swore. "Now, come on. If we get lucky, we might catch the next bus."

They made it to the stop in time to see the bus they needed leave without them, but that was okay. It wasn't far to the downtown hub, and it was all downhill anyway. The day was warmish again, sunny but breezy in that schizophrenic summer way, and it was dry.

As they trekked toward the hub, Trick demanded the mermaid details.

"There's more fantasy stuff in Fremont than just the troll statue," she informed him. "They have a bunch of weird neon signs, including some swimming and diving ladies — *mermaids*. Supposedly some fairy tale strings it all together, but I don't know if that's true or not. Me and Libby wrote some of it into our Princess X stories, back in the day."

"I still have no idea what you're talking about."

"You act like you've never even *been* there," she said in exasperation. "Hear me out, okay? It's not *just* the troll's directions to go find the mermaids . . . it's the Candy Apple Potion. *That's* the Easter egg Libby was giving me."

"Do I even want to know what a candy apple potion is?"

She launched into pitch mode, talking with her hands like he did when he was excited. "Okay: When me and Libby were kids, we weren't allowed to wear real makeup, but lip gloss was all right. Our favorite was some drugstore brand that Walgreens doesn't make anymore, but the color was called Candy Apple Potion, just like the troll says. And *that's* how I know we'll find the mermaids in Fremont. It's a detail nobody would pick up, except *me.*"

"I guess it's worth a shot." He sounded like he was game, maybe . . . but May suspected that he was still thinking about his compromised computer. Guys and their one-track minds.

They stepped outside the restaurant and ducked around a big, shiny hybrid SUV that was illegally parked in front of a fire hydrant. May wished the driver all the karma of a parking ticket, kicked the tire as she walked past, and sat down at the bus stop halfway down the block.

The bus showed up either five minutes early or five minutes late, but definitely not on time — not that either one of them complained about it. They climbed inside and went to the back row, then plopped down to wait out the trip.

Out the window, May saw the SUV. Or maybe it was only a similar model, it was hard to say . . . but it was slinking into traffic behind the bus. She almost said something to Trick, but changed her mind. It was probably nothing.

In another half hour, they rolled into Fremont. The neighborhood had character, as May's dad would say. It was built all over a set of sharp hills — so everything was all jumbled up, like all the shops and restaurants and coffeehouses were stacked on top of one another. Right on the median at the first main intersection, there was a ridiculous signpost claiming that Fremont was the center of the universe, offering estimated distances to a number of far-off places both real and fictional. And there was actually a troll under one of the bridges — a sculpture made of stone or concrete, about the size of a one-car garage.

Big enough to pick up a Volkswagen in one hand, anyway, because that's what it was doing, forever stuck in a HULK SMASH pose that delighted tourists and made locals roll their eyes.

Trick decided he wanted to go see the troll first, and since it was only a couple of blocks away from the neon swimmer signs, May let him have his way. "You never know," he said. "There could be a secret mark or something. Another Easter egg lighting the way forward. Just . . . let's go have a look, okay?"

"But I already *found* the Easter egg."

He shook his head and grinned a little, the first grin of the day, as far as she could tell. "What have you got against the troll, anyway? Don't tell me you're too old to have fun climbing on a troll."

"Right now? Yes, I am, dude."

"Stop calling me dude. It's driving me crazy."

The sculpture in question loomed over Fremont from the underside of the interstate bridge, car in hand. It was blank-faced and kind of cool — but once you'd seen it, you'd seen it. And May had seen it.

"Come on, let's skip this," she begged. "Look, there are a bunch of people up there."

"That's the best way to be inconspicuous. Find a crowd."

He started tromping up the hill, and she followed him, every bit as grumpy now as he had been at brunch.

There was nothing new or exciting there to her eyes, not even a hint of Princess X graffiti. Just a dozen or more tourists milling around the small cul-de-sac, where a perennial traffic jam turned carousel-slow so everyone got a chance to gander at the troll and snap a cell phone shot. Aside from the cars, she saw two families with little kids gleefully scaling the troll's arms, a couple of Lolita girls in fluffy black dresses, three guys dressed in business casual, eating sandwiches, and several skater kids smoking cigarettes. They nodded when another skater appeared, a tall punk with hair so blond it was almost white. He must've weighed about ninety pounds and looked a little too old to be part of the gang, but he was dressed for the part in thick eyeliner and ripped-up black clothes that fit him tighter than a mummy's wrappings.

May didn't mean to stare at him. He was good-looking, but that wasn't it. There was something odd about him, and whatever it was, she couldn't put her finger on it.

She looked away, gazing at Trick instead. But then people probably thought they were a couple, and that wasn't cool, so she changed her mind and watched the sidewalk cracks pass as they scaled the hill. When she looked up again, the skinny guy in black was gone.

When they got to the top, she asked, "What are we *really* looking for? The swimmers are back the other way."

"You want to know what I'm *really* looking for?" he answered quietly. "We're really here because of a lead I got when I went digging into the spyware on my system. This guy . . . this, um, hacker-type dude I know. He called the program that's infected my machine a trolljan."

"A . . . a trolljan?"

His eyes meticulously scanned the underside of the bridge, the troll itself, the VW in danger of being smashed . . . He was cataloging everything in the vicinity. "It's a bad pun on *Trojan*, I assume. Like the Trojan horse, you know? And like a Trojan virus, the kind that sneaks onto your computer and lets other people have access to your stuff. You gave me the idea at brunch — and since you wanted to come to Fremont anyway, I thought maybe we should check it out."

"Okay, so we've checked it out. There's nothing here," she declared firmly. "So let's go chase a better lead."

But in the back of her head, she was still thinking of that skinny guy in the eyeliner and tattered clothes. He looked nothing like the Needle Man, but maybe the Needle Man didn't work alone.

Trick walked all around the troll statue before coming back to her. "All right, I give up," he said at last. "Let's go."

FIFTEEN

As they trudged away from the troll, May kept her eyes peeled for any sign of people who might be up to no good; and the way Trick shifted his gaze back and forth told her that he was doing the same thing. They were both on edge. Maybe May was *more* on edge now because of this whole "trolljan" business. It was creepy to think someone was spying on them.

Or maybe she was antsy because Libby felt so close. After all, May had found the first key, and there were only two more keys to go before the gray child. So, yes, Libby was definitely close — for the first time since before she was buried.

Or since the Needle Man's daughter was buried in her place.

May stuffed her hands in her pockets. She would've bet her soul that the body in Libby's grave belonged to that other girl. She wondered what her name was. She wondered if the girl had ever known that her father was evil. Then she wondered if it *was* evil, really — wanting to save your kid at any price. Even the price of someone else's life.

Yes, it's evil, she decided. *It's evil because it cost me Libby.*

Furthermore, the Needle Man had definitely cost Libby her mom, probably her dad, and her freedom too. And the way things were going, you never know — it could still end up costing May's life, or Trick's, or Libby's *again*, if they could even find her.

"What?" Trick asked her.

"*What* what? I didn't say anything."

"You're frowning like you're thinking about people kicking cats or punching babies or something." He shrugged and shoved his hands into his pockets, so now both of them were doing it. Like they were trying to match.

May didn't want to match. She pulled her hands out of her jacket, flicked pieces of pocket lint off her fingernails, and said, "Fine. I was thinking that if you get me killed, I'm never going to forgive you."

"You're just mad because I didn't tell you about the trolljan before we came here."

"I don't like wild goose chases."

"But this one . . ." He popped his own hands free so he could wave them around for leisurely emphasis. "This one wasn't a chase. It was just a short detour. No harm, no foul."

"Yeah, at least it was short," she said. "Come on . . . this way. The neon signs with the swimming ladies are right over here — along the main drag."

"I find it very weird that I've never noticed any neon signs."

"They're not like . . . advertising signs," May said slowly. "They're not spelling out anything, like an old-fashioned diner, or blinking on and off like in Vegas. These are just . . . pictures. There's a couple of people dancing, and a woman diving, and a rocket ship. Stuff like that, scattered around the neighborhood. Hiding in plain sight, until it's not even hiding anymore — it's just part of the background."

They crossed the intersection, and another block or two down on the right, May pointed out the dancers: a man and woman dressed in ballroom clothes, with perfect posture. They overlooked a dive bar and a hole-in-the-wall coffee shop, but as far as she knew, the dancers didn't have anything to do with either one of them. They'd been there as long as anybody remembered, and nobody had any idea why.

"*That's* what I'm talking about." She nodded toward them. "They're more like artwork than signs. But there's a bunch of them around here. A bicycle, someplace, and a bottle of wine with a glass."

"And," he exclaimed, positively dashing to the end of the block, "a diving lady!"

He skipped over an alley and went to stand underneath the sign: one long, lean line in a blue bathing suit and a yellow swimming cap, like divers wear for the Olympics. Her hands were pointed perfectly down toward the sidewalk, and her toes were aimed at the sky.

"That's her!" May agreed, jogging forward to join him. "A mermaid." They both stared up at the diver's hands, right above their heads. Then she looked down at her own two feet. "Do you think she's pointing at something? Buried here, under the sidewalk?"

Trick frowned and shook his head. "It doesn't look like anyone's dug up this sidewalk since before we were born. Or repaired it either. I don't know . . . This doesn't feel right."

"It's not looking like a winner," May agreed, crouching down to poke around the edges of the sidewalk slab just in case. She worked her fingers into the dirt as far as she could reach, but didn't feel anything out of the ordinary. Just mud, a snail or two, and some pebbles. "But then again, neither did Black Tazza at first."

"At least no one was watching us trespass around Black Tazza. We should . . . um . . . probably leave," Trick said. May glanced up and followed his gaze past her reflection in the restaurant window. "Those people in there look like they're about to call the cops on us."

She wiped her hands on her jeans. "We can't go yet. This *is* the right place," she insisted. "Maybe it's just not . . . I don't know. Not *exactly* the right place."

"Come on. There's a coffeehouse down the block. We can get some java and brainstorm . . ."

But the last part of *brainstorm* dragged out too long, and May looked up to see whatever had snagged his attention. He was watching a dark-gray SUV roll silently toward them on the street, just a few yards away. It was a hybrid, the same model and color as the one May had seen on Capitol Hill, before they got on the bus, and it moved so quietly that it creeped her out. Given the way the windshield was tinted, and the way the sky reflected down onto the road, she couldn't see who was inside.

It looked like nobody was. It looked like a ghost car, and it sounded like one too.

And it was quite a coincidence, wasn't it? Except May didn't really believe in coincidences, did she?

She glanced up at the stoplight just behind them and saw that the light was green — but the SUV didn't speed up. It slowed down further until it pulled up right alongside them.

May took Trick by the upper arm.

"Is this some friend of yours?" he asked.

"No. Be cool," she urged.

They didn't wait for the window to roll down or anything like that; they just turned around and walked, steadily but not too fast, back toward the coffeehouse Trick had suggested in the first place, in the opposite direction from the SUV. May's grip on his arm was a little tight, a little nervous. She struggled to keep from looking back at the SUV.

"It's just a car. It's probably nothing. We're probably overreacting."

"Probably," he agreed, his mouth set in a line. "But this is weird."

"You want to know what makes it weirder? I think that guy followed us here from the Hill."

"What? Seriously?"

She didn't answer. In the reflection of a store window, she could see that the SUV was still back there, right up against the curb, blocking traffic. She couldn't stop herself — she took a quick glance over her shoulder, just in time to see a silver sedan whip around past it. Its driver made a rude gesture at the SUV as he went by.

As soon as the sedan was out of the way, the dark SUV lurched into gear. Its tires spun in a loud squeal, and the big, heavy vehicle did a hard U-turn that caught its back wheel on the sidewalk, spraying dirt and grass around as it launched forward and then headlong down the street toward them.

Trick called it before May had the chance: "Run!"

They took off, May letting go of his arm so they could both run more freely. Behind them she heard the SUV fishtail as it overcorrected, and rationally she knew that it couldn't just hop the sidewalk and run them over, because for one thing, it would have to cross two lanes of oncoming traffic to do so. But that's just what it DID do — and then it ran one red light, and then another one, chasing them the whole time.

"This way!" May darted to the left, down a cross street and toward the big empty lot where they sometimes showed movies in the summer. The SUV skidded smoothly around the corner, cutting off two oncoming cars and hopping the sidewalk before it righted itself and resumed the chase.

A woman with a stroller screamed and shoved her baby safely onto the grass. A pack of tourists fled the block and went to hide inside a lingerie boutique. Up and down the hills they ran until May stumbled on the uneven sidewalks, and Trick caught her, and then he stumbled and she caught him in turn. She couldn't believe it. There were people everywhere, and this guy was actually chasing them in a vehicle! In Fremont! It was madness — it had to be, because only a crazy person would even *think* about it.

Never did they lose the car, not for more than a few seconds. It was both a testament to the driver's knowledge of the neighborhood and a marvel of quiet traffic. That quiet, combined with the quick-footed actions of their fellow pedestrians, kept the SUV from actually hitting anybody — or at least she didn't think it hit anyone. She *did* hear people yelling as they dashed past, and one-sided cell phone conversations that mostly went something like, "Hello, 911? I'm in Fremont and there's some drunk guy driving on the sidewalks. . . . He almost flattened a baby. . . ."

May was running out of breath and she badly needed a break, but the SUV wasn't having it. They'd shake the driver on one block, and then pick him up on the next — even when they doubled back and cut through stores.

"Maybe we should, we should," she panted, "hide in one of these shops. . . ."

He shook his head no, and she knew he was right — they had to lose the guy, not lead him into a place where he could go on foot and corner them. Trick started to drag her uphill again, back toward the troll, but she jerked away and said, "No, I can't." Those were the only three words she could cough out. She couldn't run much farther, much less uphill.

A knot of traffic bought them thirty seconds at most; the SUV was trapped at a big triangular intersection. But they were stuck out in the open, on the street, and the SUV was already creeping up the side, looking to ride the walkways around the knot of traffic and keep coming for them after all, with the tenacity of the living dead.

"Did you see," Trick gasped, "that the SUV ... it doesn't have a license plate?"

"No," she gasped in return. She looked left, and right, and then behind them. She thought she heard sirens in the distance, but that didn't mean anything. It could've been ambulances or fire trucks. It might not have been cops, and even if it *did* mean cops coming for this guy, they wouldn't make it to May and Trick before the SUV did.

Then she looked back to the right again, and saw something that took the last of her breath away.

It was that guy: the tall skinny guy with the white-blond hair and the black mummy clothes. He stood at the edge of the bridge, looking dead at her. When he realized she'd seen him, he waved his hand, summoning her closer — and then he vanished around the side of the block.

It was a gamble, and she didn't have long to decide, but he wasn't chasing her with a car, so that gave him a leg up in her estimation. If ever there was a time to roll the dice, this was surely it.

"Forget it," she muttered. "Trick! Over here!" A desperate second wind gave her just enough juice to smack him on the arm and start running again.

"Toward the lake?"

"Yes, toward the lake!" It was downhill, and that was a blessing. It was not far away, and that was a blessing too.

"What are we doing?" Trick asked, with a note of panic in his voice. The traffic was untangling, and the SUV surely wasn't done with them yet. "What are you looking for?"

"I'm not sure . . ."

Then May froze, looking at the lights and the grates on the bridge, as a bus droned past her, blowing warm air up into her face. She blinked, wiped at her eyes, and said, "*Her.* I was looking for *her.* And there she is . . ."

A second diving lady, very similar to the first — outlined in neon, with her modest suit and bathing cap. She was perched on the bridge, as if she were headed over the side and into the canal.

And May saw something else too — a flash of black and blond, sliding down the bank.

She took Trick's hand. It was clammy and hot, just like hers. "This way." She dragged him off the street, down away from Fremont, and down the embankment. The wet grass under her feet gave way to big rocks, and down by the water she saw boats tied up — houseboats, sailboats, skiffs and fishers and rafts. This was no place for a car, but they could disappear into the water if they had to, just like Princess X did.

"No, not that way," Trick said. "Let's save the water for a last resort. Go *up.*"

He was right, because May was letting gravity and her own exhaustion drag her down to the water's edge, and that wasn't what they needed. It wasn't where the diving lady was aimed — she could see that now, from her new vantage spot *almost* underneath the bridge.

The diving lady pointed to a little landing, where the pillars and posts were reinforced for the drawbridge mechanism. The white-haired punk stood there, seemingly waiting. He gave them a little salute, stepped back under the bridge, and vanished.

Up above, she heard more sirens, and she could see flecks of blue and white lights punching hard, up and down along the bridge. "The SUV . . . ? Do you think they stopped it?"

"They must have, right? The cops showed up, and he can't come down to the lakeside anyway, not even with four-wheel drive," he said with more confidence than May felt. "He's got to be gone."

She scanned the edge of the neighborhood above them, not trusting Trick's powers of observation, and not trusting her own. Not trusting the SUV or its driver to be scared off by police — not a driver so crazy that he'd go on a rampage in a busy neighborhood in the middle of the day. But the longer she looked, and the longer she didn't see anything, the longer she had to catch her breath.

Finally, Trick asked, "Who was that dude in black?"

And she said, "I don't know, but he was trying to help us, I'm pretty sure. And he definitely pointed us at the other mermaid. Diving lady. Whatever. So where'd he run off to?"

"I don't see him." Trick shaded his eyes with his hand and looked all around. "But let's go find out what he wanted to show us."

"Okay. I'm right behind you," she declared.

She wasn't quite as cooled off as he was, not yet — not quite so ready to hike any farther, over the rocks and up onto the bridge's pilings. But she did it anyway, hauling herself up onto the concrete landing right below the diving lady.

There was still no sign of the white-haired punk guy. But a princess stencil with the red Chucks and purple sword was sprayed right on the metal latticework of the bridge's underpinning. May reached out to touch it, and some of the paint came off on her fingers. It was fresh — so fresh she could still smell it, despite the breeze and the scent of diesel fumes and old bait and bird poop wafting up from the water below.

"He just did this. Just now." She reached in between the metal strips of the latticework, bending her arm to keep from whacking herself on rivets and bolts the size of her fist, and felt around blindly until she found something flat, smooth, and square wedged in there.

With a little more maneuvering, she pulled free a pouch wrapped in plastic and duct tape, just like the mask in the toilet tank was. But this package was bigger. Firmer. Heavier. Maybe the size of a social studies textbook. May ran her hands over it, trying to read it like braille. She wanted to rip it open then and there, but she felt she couldn't, not when police cars were swarming above them, and there was someone out to get them. Not even though they had someone helping them too —

someone who knew about Princess X and the clues, and was willing to lead them away from danger.

But still. It felt too strange, when there were so many eyes trying to watch. She shoved the package into her messenger bag, closed the flap, and fastened it.

The rest of the way up the hill, neither May nor Trick said much. They were both keeping a lookout for the punk guy in black, but he was long gone.

Up on the bridge, they passed the SUV with all its doors opened. It was abandoned, except for the half dozen cops who swarmed it like ants.

May didn't feel very good about that. It meant the driver was on foot now. It meant he could go anywhere they could go, and chase them anywhere they could run. And they still had no idea what he looked like.

When they finally caught their bus and climbed inside, it was empty except for a pair of little old ladies and a small pack of summer students arguing about a term paper. Trick and May ducked into the back row.

"That guy . . ." he said.

"That guy . . ." May echoed. And suddenly, she knew who the punk was, and she knew who had sent him. A big fat grin ate up her face. "I bet you a million dollars, that guy was the jackdaw!"

"Oh, crap, I bet you're right," he muttered in response. "He's the stupid *bird*."

SIXTEEN

While May stared out the bus window, Trick pulled out his smartphone and logged into Gmail, making himself visible in the chat feature. BLACKBIRDWHITE was visible too — a green dot alight beside the handle.

ZHATTRICKZ: That was you, wasn't it? You helped us just now.

BLACKBIRDWHITE: Somebody had to. You're terrible at this — and I was right. You're on his radar now, and he won't stop coming.

ZHATTRICKZ: My friend said she saw his car on Capitol Hill. She thinks he followed us.

BLACKBIRDWHITE: She's probably right. You're not exactly in Witness Protection. It took me thirty seconds to find your address, and maybe ten minutes to pick you two out of a crowd.

ZHATTRICKZ: You followed us too?

BLACKBIRDWHITE: Lucky for you, yes. And lucky for me, you're bad at shaking a tail. Also lucky for you, I recognized your friend. We've been looking for her — that's why I left the package behind.

ZHATTRICKZ: Thanks, I guess. So what do we do now?

BLACKBIRDWHITE: You pass one more test. Or *she* does, anyway. The passcode you'll need is an old locker combination. If she knows it, you're in.

The green dot went dark.

May looked away from the window and saw Trick on his phone. "Anything important?"

"Nah," he told her, putting the phone away. "Text from my mom. Just telling her that everything was fine, and I'd be home for supper in a couple of hours."

"She believed you?"

"Why wouldn't she?" He shrugged. Then, to distract her, he added, "Look, here comes our stop."

SEVENTEEN

They didn't go home. Not right away.

"I must be getting paranoid," May confessed as they got coffee at a shop not far from their apartment building. She clutched the package and ran her fingers over its contours, like she was trying to guess the contents of a wrapped Christmas present. "But then again, that guy tried to *kill* us."

Trick handed her a couple packets of yellow sweetener and stirred his own drink with a straw. "We don't know that. Not for sure."

"He tried to *run us over with his car.*"

He blew a resigned sigh into his coffee. "Maybe. And maybe it's time to get the cops involved. If our lives are in danger, we'd be stupid not to tell them, you know?"

"But say we *do* go to the police . . . what do we tell them? That we've been breaking and entering and doing all sorts of things we probably shouldn't in order to prove somebody's death was faked three years ago? I'm sure that'll go over *great*. They totally won't throw us into juvie just for wasting their time. Besides, going to the cops worked out real well for Princess X, didn't it?"

"That was fiction. This is real life," Trick insisted.

"Was it, really? I bet Libby really did try to get help from the police, and I bet the Needle Man — whoever he is — reported her as a runaway or something like that. I bet that part totally happened, just like the bit with her dad."

"Well, fine — you're probably right about that much," he conceded. "But I don't think they'd arrest us just for asking questions or trying to file a report. This is starting to freak me out. Usually, at worst, people online threaten to give me a beatdown. They're always fat guys in their underpants, living in their parents' basements, so no beatdown is ever going to occur, and we all know it. But here in meatspace? This is *different*. This is crazy."

May picked at the tape on the package in her lap. She almost had one good corner lifted up and ready to pull. "You're not wrong, but we're getting close to finding Libby. Really close. The police will only get in our way."

He blew another gusty sigh onto his coffee, deemed it cooled enough to try, and took a sip. "So are you going to open that package, or just feel it up all afternoon?"

"I'm *working* on it," she said. "It's a lot of tape, okay? If you're that impatient, hook me up with that pocketknife again." But before he had time to oblige, the corner she'd loosened gave way, so she said, "Never mind" — and with a hearty yank she loosed the tape in one long, sticky, unspooling line. Inside was an oversize envelope made of some weirdly thin, durable material, but there was a pull tab on top, and it opened easily enough.

"And what do we have here?" Trick craned his neck to get a better look over the table.

"It's a laptop sleeve." A red flannel one, soft to the touch. A round black button fastened its flap at one end. She unbuttoned it quickly and gently spilled the contents onto the table.

"A laptop sleeve with a tablet inside," he observed. He snatched it up before May could stop him. "An iPad, several years old, with a red vinyl skin. It's not the newest model by a long shot. Not the fanciest, either — but serviceable, I guess. So *this* is the red box made of lightning and glass."

"Give it back," May commanded.

"Nothing's written on it or drawn on it. The good stuff must be inside. Turn it on," he urged as he reluctantly passed it back to her.

Her thumb smushed the power button. It booted up quickly to a home screen with a simple wallpaper: an ordinary school locker affixed with a simple padlock.

"It's charged up?" Trick asked.

"It's got enough power to run," she said, checking the little battery icon.

He drew his chair around the small table to sit right next to her. "Then it's been plugged in recently; those old units don't hold their juice very well. Is it passcode-protected?"

"Yes, but this one's easy."

"It is?"

"Give a girl some space here," she said, using her elbow for emphasis. "Watch this . . ."

Carefully she typed the numbers 1, 9, 2, and 8.

"And that's . . . ?"

"Nineteen, two, eight. Our old locker combination," she declared as the lock screen vanished.

"Wow. Go *you*. This jackdaw guy must've known we were coming for it. He must've had it on him, and slipped it into place just before we got there."

She looked up. "But how?"

Trick looked a little twitchy, like there was something he wasn't telling her. But before she could corner him on it, he shrugged. "I don't know. Now show me what's on it. I want to see."

May wanted to see too, so she let the subject go. She drew her fingers lightly across the tablet, touching the icons without activating them. "There's not much here. Basic functions, you know. Calendar and clock, newsstand, that kind of thing." Now she tapped them, one after the other. "But they're all empty."

Trick made grabby-hands at the device, and May fended him off while still poking at the screen. "Why would someone leave us a blank iPad?" she asked, more as a rhetorical question than a real one. "There must be *something* on here."

"I'm sure you're right . . ." he said, still seeking a way past her defenses. "If you'd just give it to me, I know how to look a little more closely."

Eventually, she handed it to him. "I thought you were a Microsoft guy."

"Oh, I *am*. Windows is my friend," he told her. "But you know what they say about keeping your friends close and your enemies closer."

"You have a really warped relationship with technology."

"You're not the first to say so. Hey, look, here we go. A couple of files hidden in one of the minor app icons."

"Where? What are they?"

"Hang on," he mumbled, fingers dashing around the touch screen. "Okay. This one's just a JPEG. Here you go."

Trick turned the tablet sideways, and the image filled the screen.

MAYBE SHE DOES, AND MAYBE SHE DOESN'T.

BUT WHEREVER THE FIRST PRINCESS RESTS, IT ISN'T HERE.

NEVER MIND THE ASHES. YOU'LL FIND THE BLACK MIRROR INSIDE HER GREEN CUP. YOU'LL NEED IT, IF YOU WANT TO DEFEAT THE NEEDLE MAN. YOU'LL NEED EVERY BIT OF LEVERAGE YOU CAN GET.

"Trick, you've read the whole comic, right?"

"I sat down with it last night, and yeah — I think I'm all caught up through the end."

She crooked her neck and squinted at the image. "Is this page online?"

"Nope, I don't think so."

They saw it at the same time: At the bottom of the last panel, in a font so tiny, Trick had to pinch it to make it bigger, waited a URL.

"Can you click it?" May asked, already jabbing her finger toward it, just in case.

"No, it's just written onto the image; it's not a link. Give me a pen, would you?"

She fished around in her bag until she found one, and grabbed the nearest napkin. "Read it off to me," she ordered, and he obliged. The address was a long one, mostly numbers, except for *Dropbox* after the introductory bit.

While Trick looked up the coffeehouse's WiFi and waited for the Internet browser to load, May asked him, "What's that — Dropbox?"

"It's a storage site, basically, and this address means someone's hosting a file there." He connected the tablet to the public WiFi and meticulously, laboriously entered the URL.

A page loaded.

It was another JPEG, a simple image of scanned material — both sides of a driver's license, and both sides of a work ID badge, both belonging to Kenneth Mullins, a name that Trick and May breathed out loud in perfect sync. Then Trick added, reading the ID, "He's a tech guy for the University of Washington's medical center. Or he was, back in 2008."

"You were right about him being a geek. And this means he'd *definitely* have the know-how to rig all this stuff together."

"Maybe." Trick dragged his fingers around the screen, moving the image up and down, enlarging it here and there. "Maybe he was useful IT, maybe he was just there to answer the phones. Not everybody in a headset knows anything."

"He looks . . ." She stared down at the tiny squares with Kenneth Mullins's face in them. He was a brown-haired white guy, probably about her dad's age. "*Normal.*"

"The scary ones always do."

"That's what they say every time they catch a serial killer. Either nobody's paying attention . . . or 'normal' is much, much worse than everybody thinks." May hugged herself without particularly noticing it.

"I need to get home," Trick muttered.

"What?"

"You heard me," he said a little louder. "Come on, you're invited too. This won't take long, but I need my own system to try it."

"What won't take long? Try what?"

He handed her the tablet. "I'll explain on the way."

May stuffed the device back into its sleeve, and then into her messenger bag. She halfway bused the table on her way out the door. Because they were only a block or two from home, Trick's explanations waited until they were riding alone in the world's slowest elevator, crawling up toward his floor. "Even *if*," he said, watching the lighted numerals tick past, "we don't have enough information to figure out where this guy lives, we definitely have enough to find his daughter's grave."

"We have his driver's license."

"From 2008. I'd be stunned if he still lived on South Mercer Street. I bet you he lives out on Bainbridge Island. But his daughter's grave . . . that's probably someplace closer. And *that's* where the comic on the tablet is pointing us."

"You want to find her grave?" May was unsurprised, but lightly appalled. She tried to keep an open mind about grave robbing, but she failed on the grounds of *yuck*, and also because digging in public places tended to attract attention.

"Of course. The comic said the grave is empty, and we'd find the black mirror inside her green cup."

"I've never heard of a cup-shaped coffin."

"Coffin, no." The elevator chimed. The doors opened. "But what about an urn? That's kind of cuplike. And the comic *did* say, 'Never mind the ashes.'"

"The last time it mentioned a cup, or a chalice anyhow, it turned out to be a toilet — so I guess anything's possible. Maybe you're right, maybe she was cremated. It sure would make our lives easier if that's the case."

In an unwelcome flash, she thought of Libby's funeral. Libby hadn't been cremated. She'd been buried in a silver casket. May remembered thinking that the handles on the thing alone were worth more than all of her mother's jewelry put together, and they were just going to put it into the ground and forget about it, because they *could*. It was horrible to think about a waste of money at your best friend's funeral, and she felt a little jab of shame about it, even now.

But maybe, at the time, she did it out of self-preservation, staring at the church-lamp gleam off the silver and not thinking about their locker, their matching T-shirts, or Princess X. It had been the only way she could keep it together — to focus on just that moment and not everything in her past with Libby, everything she'd lost.

Trick continued. "If we're right, and the Needle Man switched his daughter's body and Libby's, then *she's* the one buried in Libby's grave. So if Ken's daughter has a grave, there's nobody in it. No actual body, I mean." He pulled out his keys, opened the door to his apartment, announced his presence, and paused. No one greeted him back. "It's just us."

May frowned thoughtfully as she followed him inside. "But Ken had to *pretend* to do something with his own kid's body. There's no mention of her mother in the comic, so maybe she was out of the picture. . . . But surely there'd be grandparents, cousins, aunts, or uncles. There'd be *somebody*. And those somebodies might want a grave to visit."

Trick knocked the bedroom door open with his elbow. "All he would need is a bag of fireplace ash, or kitty litter, or whatever. He could just . . . *tell* people he'd had her cremated, after he'd claimed her body. I doubt anyone ever asks for a receipt." Over at his desk, he leaned behind a monitor and flipped a switch. Buttons lit up, and preliminary beeps announced that things were powering on. His workstation began to hum.

"Hey, um . . ." May pointed at the CPU tower. "Didn't you say someone had hacked your system? You were pretty ticked about it."

"I'm still pretty ticked about it, but there's not much I can do. If it's really Ken Mullins who slipped me the spyware, and if that was really him in the SUV in Fremont, then he already knows we're onto him. So, all right then, *fine*. He can watch me punch through a database or two if it makes him happy. If he knows we've got his name and personal information, he might think twice about bothering us again." He paused, and then said, "Like he said . . . I mean, um, like the Princess X page said, we've got a little bit of leverage. But it's not leverage if he doesn't know we have it."

"Maybe you should use my laptop, to be on the safe side," she tried.

"I can't. Not without a whole afternoon of downloading, installing, and configuring the programs I need. Listen," he said, turning to face her, the wheels of his chair scooting a few inches to follow his feet. "You said it yourself, this guy tried to catch us with the hood of his car. He knows what we look like. For that matter, he probably knows where we live — he could have found my place through the spyware, easy as pie. And if you're right, and he followed us out to Fremont . . . well. Right now, the best thing we can do is . . . is . . ."

"Yeah?" she asked, a little more earnestly than she liked. She wanted to hear that he had an answer on deck, because *she* sure didn't.

He swallowed hard and set his mouth in a grim line. "We have to force his hand, baby."

"This isn't a *game*, dude. And don't call me baby."

"Then stop calling me dude. But whatever we do, we'll have to do it fast. We're on foot, and riding the bus. He's got a car."

"He abandoned his car. Remember?"

"But he might've stolen another one, and I can probably find that out for sure, if you give me a minute." The chair swiveled back to face the monitors. He cracked his knuckles and started typing.

"He couldn't have stolen another car, like, *immediately*."

"I don't want to take any chances," he mumbled, but that was as close to a concession as May was going to get. "Give me the tablet. I want another look at that file."

She passed it over, sleeve and all, and watched as he double-checked Ken's license number — then carefully typed it into some window on his screen that didn't look like Google. "Is that another Dropbox link?"

"No. This is a civil records database. Technically, everything here is public info, so I'm not even breaking the law right now. Here," he said, as a column of text scrolled up, accompanied by a larger picture of Ken Mullins. "Holy crap — okay. Okay," he repeated.

May couldn't stand the uncertainty, so she hovered behind him, reading over his head. "What are we looking at?"

"His criminal record."

Her stomach sank, and her mouth went dry. "He has a criminal record?"

"A couple of speeding tickets, a fistful of parking tickets, and — wait, here's a better one." He paused his scrolling and pointed to a specific entry, a brief block of text with a police report number attached. "Someone named Linda Hall took out a restraining order against him back in 1993, but it looks like she withdrew it, or let it lapse, or whatever. And about a year later, someone named Kathy Larsen got a restraining order too, and he violated it twice. She didn't press charges, but he ended up with probation anyway."

"So he's a stalker." May fidgeted with the back of Trick's chair.

"Looks like it. Let me see what else I can find." In another minute or two, and with another page full of lists, charts, and figures, he announced, "In 1995, Ken Mullins married Elaine Akiyama."

"Akiyama . . . that's Japanese, right?"

"Sounds like it. According to this, she died a few years ago, in a car accident. And *heeeere* . . ." — he gave the revelation a hard drag on the vowels — "is a death certificate for the first princess: Christina Louise Mullins. A year and a couple of months younger than Libby. A Gemini. Dead of acute lymphocytic leukemia the day after your friend died. Or vanished. Or . . . you know what I mean."

"Leukemia. So it *was* cancer."

With a flick of his wrist, he opened another window and plugged the term into an ordinary search bar. "A kind of bone cancer, to be more precise."

"Oh God. Oh, *wow*." May's head spun. It was all falling into place — the medical records, the girl in the hospital . . . and of course, the gray child and the boat full of bones. "She died of bone cancer, and Libby was a match for the bone marrow. The princess's bones could've saved her, that's what the comic said."

"Yeah, this is pretty crazy." He was mumbling again, reading one thing while he said something else out loud. He might've said more, but just then, the phone rang — a landline there in his apartment.

"You guys have a landline?" May asked. "I thought my dad was the only man left on earth who still had one."

Trick turned away from the computer. "Yeah, we do. And lately it's been . . ." He paused as it rang, and rang, and rang, then said suddenly, sharply, "Don't answer it!"

She frowned at him. "I wasn't going to. There's probably no one on the other end anyway."

"Why would you say that?" he asked, his gaze so intense it almost alarmed her.

"Because it's been happening at my dad's place — the landline rings, and when you pick it up, nobody's there."

His eyes narrowed, and he didn't reply. Trick and May waited together until the ringing finally stopped. Then he told her, "That can't be a coincidence. It's too weird to be nothing."

"You think it's Ken?"

"He could be fishing for us, or threatening us, trying to find out if we're home. Maybe he's trying to get information from our parents, I don't know," he said, returning to his typing. "When we're finished with this, I'll dig into the phone company records. Maybe I can find out who's been calling us, and if it turns out it's just some glitch . . . great. But for now, let's handle one thing at a time and go on assuming the worst. We start with Christina's grave." He jabbed his index finger at the screen. "Her final resting place is just a box number at a crypt, so I was right and she was cremated . . . and . . . we're in luck!" he added.

"Since *when*?" May asked drolly.

"Since Ken had Christina buried over at Lake View Cemetery. It's a twenty-minute walk from here; we won't even need a bus. All we need is something to break open the crypt. I'll bring my mom's vehicle emergency kit. It's got one of those things you can use to break car windows. I bet it'll work on a crypt too."

"Why isn't it in her car?"

"She keeps forgetting it." Trick launched himself out of the chair and shot down the hall to a storage closet, where he rifled around for a few seconds. He returned with a pink canvas bag, which he set before her with a magician's flourish.

"It's pink," May said.

"Yes, it's pink. That's how you know it's for *ladies*."

"That might be the stupidest thing I've ever heard you say."

"I was being ironic."

"God, I hope so. You want me to carry it? So you won't be embarrassed?" she offered, holding out her hand.

"We don't need the whole thing, just the little hammer. It's pink too, but I'm secure in my masculinity." He smirked, found the hammer, and stuffed it into his messenger bag.

The phone rang again.

"Ignore it," he commanded once more.

"Fine, but let's get out of here," May urged. The vintage-style bell, clanging in cycles . . . It unsettled her. "That ringing is driving me nuts."

"You got the tablet?"

"I'll get it." She gathered up her things. "Okay, I'm ready."

"Let's do this fast. Lake View might be the only break we get. How fast can you run in those boots?"

"Faster than you, dude." She grinned at him.

"Then come on, baby. *Prove it*."

EIGHTEEN

"Slowpoke," May chided Trick with a wheeze as she leaned on the cemetery gate for support. Her toes were almost numb from all the pavement-pounding, and one untied bootlace trailed on the ground, damp and gross from being dragged through the grass. She bent over to tie it, conveniently hiding the fact that she was about to fall over from exhaustion.

Trick heaved himself over the curb, then changed his mind and sat down on it. "Yes," he wheezed back at her. "I *am* a slowpoke. And you were right, you're faster than me. Is that what you want to hear?"

"Hourly, if you can manage it." She grinned and wiped a smattering of afternoon drizzle off her cheeks. "Come on. Let's get this over with."

LAKE VIEW CEMETERY read the sign by the gates, and there was some other stuff too — mostly about when it was established, where the office was, and what the hours were. May and Trick still had plenty of time before the gates closed and trapped them there with the crows, the squirrels, and the cadaverous trees.

"Have you ever been here before?"

"Yes, but not in ages." Every Seattle school kid went there at some point, usually at the beginning or end of a local history class. All the city founders and the most interesting folks from the last century were buried there. She stared around, using her hand to shield her eyes from the milk-white light that seemed weirdly vivid and blank above them. "You said Christina's got a box number or something, right?"

"Right." He climbed to his feet. "I know there's a building back on the far side of the hill, so maybe that's it — kind of like a library for dead people."

"A library for dead people. I can't tell if that's cool or disgusting."

"Can't it be both?"

"I don't see why not." Her cell phone took that opportunity to ring wildly. When she looked down at the display, she said, "It's my dad. I wonder what he wants."

"Answer the phone and find out."

"Nah." She shook her head. "We won't be here long. I'll call him back when we're done."

Together, May and Trick hiked between the graves, along the narrow roads when it suited them and off in the hedges, headstones, and oversize trees when it didn't. Trick was right: On the far side of the hill's natural peak stood a long white building about the size of a small gas station. Made of white marble and open at each end with no roof to cover it all, this was indeed the open-air library of the dead (as May couldn't stop thinking of it, now that Trick had said it out loud). It was bright and clean, almost sterile. Inside, there was a bit of an echo, and nothing to see except the small rectangular nameplates telling you who belonged where.

Trick's phone rang, and the music from *Doctor Who* filled the narrow space until he could fumble it off. "Sorry," he mumbled, probably to the dead people.

"Who was it?"

"My mom."

"You didn't answer it."

"You didn't answer your dad, either."

"True," she admitted. "But grave robbing is more important than coordinating pizza toppings for later tonight. Unless . . ." She turned to him, suddenly nervous. "Unless you think something's happened. What if they need us? What if they're looking for us?"

"They're parents. They're always looking for us." His phone rang again — but he silenced the ringer and stuffed it back into his pocket. "Sometimes, Mom's the needy sort."

"Yeah, but my dad's usually . . . not so much. Hey, what was Christina's Dewey decimal number?"

"Doesn't matter," Trick said, retreating to the end of the corridor. "They aren't marked on the plaques. The ID number is probably just for the cemetery's record-keeping purposes. I'll start over here, you start over there. Speak up if you spot her."

May ran her finger along the rows of bronze plates. Some were shinier than others, but they were all the same shape and size, with a name, a date, a dash, and another date, all in the same font. Nothing personalized about any of it. It was either sad or just plain boring.

Her fingernail scraped lightly down the row, and Trick's shoes made almost the exact same sound, a little louder on the leaf-littered marble floor. She hesitated over a CHRISTINE but kept going until she could safely exclaim, "I found her!"

Trick bounded to her side. "For real?"

"For real: Christina Louise Mullins. Here she is. Allegedly."

"Bullcrappedly," he said, fishing the pink hammer out of his bag.

May offered, "You want me to do it?"

He leaned his head back so he could see past her and out into the cemetery proper. "No, I've got it." Having checked that the coast was clear, he raised the small pink hammer, picked a corner below Christina's name . . . and then abruptly stopped himself.

May looked over her shoulder. "What are you doing? Get cracking, would you?"

"Someone beat us to it. Look here, see? There's a crack . . ."

May poked it with her finger. The chunk shifted, very slightly. "Give me the hammer," she said, snapping her fingers.

"Because it's pink?"

"Because I want the other end, the pry-bar end. I bet we can just lift this thing out." She accepted the hammer and wedged its metal edge into the crack. With a short, gentle scrape and a pop, a triangle-shaped piece dropped free. Trick caught it before it hit the floor. Barely.

A few dusty chunks of filler tinkled down, powdering everything with white. May squeezed her hand into the hole. She didn't know what she expected to find back there — hopefully, not mice or roaches — but her fingertips grazed a smooth, curved shape. "I feel the urn."

"Well, you can't pull it out through that hole, can you?"

"No, smart aleck, I can't. However . . ." She leaned against the flat, blank wall of plaques and marble and levered her hand against the broken stone, pulling it forward. It gave a tiny bit at first, and then more. Finally, with a great screeching squeal, the front slab left its resting place.

May and Trick caught it together, which was good — it was heavier than it looked. They set it down carefully, both of them looking back and forth between the two entrances at either end, hoping and praying that no one had seen them, that no one had heard them, that no one was watching.

The intermittent buzz of May's silenced cell phone hummed against the slab of stone. "It can *wait*," she said under her breath, and when Trick shot her a funny look, she said, "My dad again, I bet." She looked inside the hole. "Hey, look — the urn's green. I guess this is the green cup after all."

"I didn't even need your insider knowledge to figure this one out. The clues are definitely getting easier."

"That just means we're getting closer. It's not just the comics on the web giving us clues now. It's Jackdaw too. Libby must've sent him to help us."

"Is that what you think?"

Their hands met inside the cubbyhole, and then their eyes met too. May stared him down. "Yeah, that's what I think." She pushed his hands off the urn and withdrew it, dragging it into the cold, gray light of afternoon. She turned it over in her hands, checking the exterior for any obvious clues. It was shiny and dark, about the size of a can of paint. Its surface was glossy emerald green, and it had brass trim and hardware.

She held it up beside her head and gave it a little shake. "I hear something knocking around inside. You still have that pocketknife?"

"It's a *multitool*," he reminded her for the millionth time. He dug it out of his messenger bag anyway.

May picked the part she wanted — not a blade but a flat-head screwdriver — and jammed it in the seam between the lid and body of the urn, wiggling the tool back and forth. The seal broke with a little sucking sound and the lid popped free, releasing a tiny puff of what May very much hoped was not *actually* the ashes of a human being.

Trick covered his face with his arm and spoke through his sleeve. "Be careful!"

"I *am* being careful! And it's not like this used to be an actual *person*," she prayed. She set the lid aside and peered down into the container. Swirls of gray that looked like smoke rose up in tiny tendrils. She held her breath to keep from breathing in any more of the stuff, whatever it was, and squinted against the dark interior.

"Just give it to me. I'll jam my hand in there. I'm not chicken."

"Your hand won't fit," she told him. "Mine won't, either."

"So what do you suggest?" he asked, but she was already carrying the urn out of the structure into the watered-down daylight — where anybody visiting the graves could see them.

May looked left, looked right, and looked back inside the corridor. She didn't see anyone except Trick, and whatever was in that urn, it wasn't Christina Mullins. She knew it, and she believed it, and there was no turning back now — Libby was *alive*, and this was another piece of proof, and maybe it was more leverage against the Needle Man. They were going to get this guy, and she was going to get Libby back, once and for all.

So she dumped the ashes onto the ground.

"Jesus!" Trick exclaimed.

"He doesn't care!" May assured him. The ashes billowed and pooled, and drifted away on every slight tug of the moist air. She kept shaking the upended urn, which produced a harsh clattering sound. She tilted the thing left and right and shifted her angle, and with another round of jostling, a slim phone in a mirrored case came tumbling out. It crashed into the ashes, and they scattered even farther, powdering the lawn in every direction.

Trick made a grab for the phone but then changed his mind, withdrawing his hand before he could reach it.

"You *are* chicken." May picked up the phone and wiped it on the grass, then on her pants, revealing the shiny chromed surface in all its glory. "And this *is* the black mirror."

"But you don't know for a fact that those *aren't* ashes."

"I'm pretty sure they *are* ashes, actually." She sneezed, sending more sooty currents fluttering aloft. "But they're from a fireplace or something. They don't taste a thing like people."

Like the tablet they'd found, the phone was two or three generations old. Pale gray detritus outlined its power button and was worked into the seams along the exterior, and no matter how many times May wiped it on her butt, it wouldn't come totally clean. When it was finally as grime-free as it was going to get, she pushed the button, swiped the indicator, and was greeted by a plain old iPhone start-up screen. There was no background picture — just the boring bubbles that come standard. And much like the tablet, it had been stripped of all the extras — no apps, no photos, no games.

"Check the contacts list," Trick suggested over her shoulder, still unwilling to touch the tainted device.

"You're a worse chicken than I thought." May pressed the appropriate icon, but before the list could present itself, a text message came chiming through.

Both of them were startled enough to jump backward. May dropped the phone in the grass, but at least she missed the ash puddle this time. She lunged forward and retrieved it, but the text had already faded from the screen, so she jabbed the icon that would display incoming messages.

Three words popped up: DON'T GO HOME.

Then a second text: YOUR PLACE IS ON THE NEWS.

Silently, they stared at the messages, reading them again and again. Then Trick noted, "The phone doesn't recognize the number, but there aren't any contacts — so that's no surprise."

"It's *got* to be the jackdaw."

May's own phone was buzzing again, and so was Trick's. She checked her screen and saw that her dad had called seven times in the last hour, and here he was, calling again. If her apartment was on the local news, she wanted to know why. Trick pulled out his phone at the same time. They stepped away from each other and accepted their calls.

"Dad?" she said.

"Mom?" she heard, as Trick answered the phone behind her.

Her dad sounded just short of frantic. "Where the hell are you?"

"I'm . . . I'm out with Trick." She tried to sound casual, and she surely fooled no one. "Killing time. We just finished up some coffee and hot chocolate."

"Don't give me that — I saw you on the news! You and that kid, that friend of yours, you were running away from a car in Fremont. Is that where you are right now? I'll come and get you."

"No, Dad. No, we're back on Cap Hill. How did you, um . . . how did you know about that? And why is our place on the news?"

"That car, rampaging through Fremont. About a dozen people got cell phone footage of it, and it's been all over TV for the last hour. I called the cops when I recognized you, right about the time one of that kid's teachers ID'd him. So now the police are looking for you both."

"Why would the police want us? We didn't do anything!"

"That guy who was chasing you, he ran into some woman by the church and then knocked over a kid walking her dog. People got hurt, and he got away. Does this . . ." He shifted his grip on the phone; May could hear the fabric of his shirt rubbing against the microphone. "Does this have something to do with Princess X? Tell me the truth, May."

She could feel herself flushing, hot and unhappy. Embarrassed, though she wasn't entirely sure why — maybe it was the idea of being on TV and not even knowing about it. She hoped her hair looked good. "The truth is . . ." she started to say.

Behind her, it sounded like Trick was having a similar conversation with his mother. "Mom, calm down. We're fine. Everything's fine. Every*body*'s fine." Pause. "Okay, maybe not *those* people, but me and May . . . we're okay. What do you mean Jim's in the hospital?"

May held her phone against her chest, hoping her dad couldn't hear. "Hospital? Someone's in the hospital?"

"My mom's boyfriend," he half whispered, half mouthed at her. "Someone broke in to our apartment."

She pulled her phone back up to her ear. Her dad was midsentence, but she hardly heard him. ". . . where you are, and I'll come get you. Something bad is going on, and I wish you'd just talk to me if you're in some kind of trouble."

"I'm not . . . not in trouble, exactly," she murmured, still trying to listen in on the other conversation.

Trick was struggling to get a word in edgewise. "But he's going to be okay, right? Good, I'm glad. But I want you to answer my question: *Is my computer okay?*"

May's dad wanted to know, "What does 'exactly' mean?"

Trick was having a meltdown now. "What happened? How bad is it? What did they get? Okay, fine — what did they *break*?"

"Dad," she said slowly, interrupting him in the middle of his tirade, but that was fine, because she'd missed most of it anyway. "Dad, did someone break in to our apartment?"

"No, but there was a robbery in the building. The paramedics took someone away on a stretcher. It nearly gave me a heart attack."

"But it didn't, right? You're okay?"

"Me? I'm fine. Don't worry about me. It's my job to worry about *you*. I've been trying to call you for an hour. Maybe you don't need a phone if you're not going to answer when I try to reach you."

"That's just crazy talk," she said with an awkward little laugh. "And I *did* answer, eventually. I'm sorry, I swear."

"May?" His voice held a note of warning. "You need to come home. Right now."

"I can't," she breathed.

"You'd damn well better, young lady —" His voice cut off sharply. To someone else, he said, "Yes, I've got her. She's safe. She's out with that other kid, Patrick."

"Dad, I *can't* come home," she said again, stronger this time. "Not yet."

"Why not yet?"

"Libby's alive, Dad — she's alive and I'm going to find her. I'm going to save her."

"May, don't do this."

"Just so you know, the Needle Man is real, and we've almost got him." And before she could talk herself out of it, before she could hear any further arguments to the contrary . . . before she could start yelling or crying, or telling him to trust her . . . she took a deep breath and hung up. She turned off the phone and faced Trick, who had already done the same. He looked as pale as the ashes from the urn, every bit as rattled as May.

"Well?"

"Well . . ." he replied. "Jackdaw's right, assuming he's the one who left us the phone. We can't go home. My mom's boyfriend got stabbed, and Ken took my CPU."

May's hands were shaking, and she hadn't even noticed. She wiped her own phone on her arm. "Then what do we do? Where do we go?"

The other phone gave her the answer in another text message. LEAVE THE TABLET IN CM'S SLOT.

"Here? We should leave it here?" May asked the phone, or Trick, or herself. "That can't be right. It's proof! It's leverage!"

"I don't know, May. I think the bird is right," Trick said. "It's got that comic, and the Dropbox link to all Ken's personal info. If he catches us, it's something he can take away from us and destroy."

"I *guess* we could leave it here," she relented. "My dad knows we're investigating the whole Princess X thing, and maybe he doesn't believe that Libby's still alive — but he knows her mom was murdered. If we give him this stuff, he'll know what it's about. And if something happens to us, he can give it to the police."

"Maybe it's not as much leverage as we want, but . . . if something happens to us," he echoed with a gulp, "it's insurance."

"I can . . . I can send Dad a text message, and tell him where to look. Just in case."

They stood there a moment, then collected the tablet from May's messenger bag. They shoved it into the slot beside the urn, and together, they replaced the heavy stone cover — even though it now had a chunk missing.

When they were done, May took the phone and replied to the text: DONE. NOW WHAT, JACKDAW? WHERE DO WE FIND YOU? WHERE DO I FIND LIBBY?

And he replied: KING STREET STATION.

NINETEEN

First, there was Jacob Raykes.

Since birth, he was so ghastly pale and silvery blond that everyone assumed it had to be fake, or some kind of medical condition. When he reached high school, the other students called him creep, goth, and queer. He yelled back that they were right about all three, but they'd left out *genius*.

And he *was* a genius. The proper kind, the gifted, golden kind who get scholarships and grants, who collect perfect scores on tests that are supposed to be unperfectable.

How he hated it all.

College meant nothing to him, and it never would. His father said he could move right out if he was going to like other boys like that, and his mother said maybe if he only got an ordinary job or a haircut, or traveled the world a little bit, he'd be able to "find himself." She was gentler on him, for all that gentleness mattered.

He stayed home for a while, because what else could he do? He was seventeen and broke, crashed out of high school without a diploma. Too strange to go, and too uncomfortable to stay where he was, he spent all his time on the Internet. Within a year he knew almost everything about the web and about the world — and that's how he "found himself."

Because his mother couldn't make him stay, and his father didn't care to keep him, he threw his tech into a backpack with a couple pairs of pants and three white shirts he'd defaced with a Sharpie, and he left.

He went wherever he wanted, but mostly stayed near Puget Sound. He panhandled when he was hungry, made a few friends with empty couches for when it got too cold, and learned how to barter his time and his skills to set up websites for activists like himself — people with big ideas and small wallets, because, it turned out, genius had fewer practical applications than he'd ever suspected.

Then he discovered the joys of advertising. Online ads weren't a gold mine, but with a few well-placed lines of code, he could eat three meals a day and score a warmer coat from the Crossroads secondhand shop on Broadway. With a little bit of stability and a growing network of fellow ne'er-do-wells, he turned his attention to politics.

Before long, Jacob had cobbled together a no-frills webzine dedicated to the radical anarchist principles that felt right to him. He called it *All Free Peoples*. He built it on borrowed and sometimes stolen equipment, and borrowed and sometimes stolen wireless Internet — and there, he published whoever and whatever he wanted.

On his twentieth birthday, he did not answer his mother's email asking for a phone number. Instead, he went to a buddy of his who owed him a favor. This buddy's name was Spencer, but everyone called him Hawk, so Jacob knew he'd understand. With a sewing needle and a pot of ink, Hawk tattooed a small black bird on Jacob's left wrist, and from that day forward, he answered only to Jackdaw.

Jackdaw set up a tiny kingdom on Pioneer Square, in the old part of Seattle that was highly historical and somewhat protected. Mostly, historical protection meant only that nobody had torn it down yet; and sometimes, if a building was lucky, it got gutted and turned into office space rather than leveled.

The Starfish was a luckier building still. Long ago, a hotel — then apartments, then warehousing space, then lofts, then nothing at all — the Starfish was big enough to quietly host a dozen or more squatters on any given day, but small enough to avoid civic notice. As long as it was quiet, and there were no visible criminal activities taking place, everyone left it alone.

But avoiding civic notice had its drawbacks, and the building was in less than stellar repair. Most of the floors tipped to the left, and many of the doors wouldn't shut right in their teetering frames. Secretly, most of the squatters knew that the next big quake would take it down — if some ridiculous developer didn't get his hands on the deed first.

Jackdaw told them not to worry. He had the city property databases at his fingertips, and now the place was held by the Songbird Trust — an entirely fictitious entity comprised of Jackdaw himself and a phony set of legal documents filed through the Internet, signed by made-up lawyers and sealed with a notary press he'd found in a Dumpster. The date on the press said it was 1987, but that was fine. It only made the effort look established rather than made up on the fly.

Because, it turned out, genius had more practical applications than he'd ever suspected.

He built a small server farm from scavenged and free-cycled equipment, much of it old-fashioned but all of it functional. Planned obsolescence was meaningless under Jackdaw's crackling fingers and sizzling code. He offered hosting space to those who wished to duck the established corporations — fellow anarchists, conspiracy theorists, and the wannabe Snowdens and Assanges of the world yet to come.

By twenty-one years of age, he'd found his stride. He'd also found a criminal record that read like a petty short list of things nobody ever went to jail for, and another half dozen tattoos. He took nothing that would kill his brain cells or interfere with his thinking. No substances that would lie to him.

Except coffee. He tolerated coffee. It kept him sharp, kept him quick, and gave him an excuse to patrol the square — watching the routes the bike cops pedaled, monitoring the usual homeless population, listening to tourists argue in a dozen languages, picking through the things people left behind. The Starbucks people knew him on sight, and they didn't charge him for his Venti cup of black drip because he'd helped out the manager once. Some crazy guy had cornered her at a bus stop, but Jackdaw had been the crazier of the two and he'd chased the other guy off. Voilà. Free coffee for life.

He was sipping some of that coffee one dank autumn afternoon, letting the steam from the small vent waft up his nose, when he felt a tug.

A tiny tug. Almost imperceptible, right where his backpack strap had worn a groove into his shoulder. It was the kind of tug you'd only notice if you'd made that kind of tug before, unzipping a pocket and hoping to strike gold before the person wearing the backpack saw what you were doing.

He pretended not to notice. He sat his coffee down on the window-sill of a fudge shop, and without looking, he snapped his hand back and caught the thief by the wrist.

"Let go of me!" she demanded.

He looked her over. She was about five and a half feet tall, a lithe, dark-haired girl probably not a day over fifteen. Asian, more or less. Hair the color of the coffee in his paper cup, cut short around her chin in a jagged way that suggested she'd done it herself. She was not quite thin enough to call gaunt, but his fingers wrapped all the way around her wrist to fold over on his own knuckles. She looked hungry — and scared as hell.

"Let go of my camera," he counteroffered. It dangled by the strap from her free hand. "It's not worth anything. You couldn't trade it for a sandwich."

Her eyes slipped to the square, heavy brick of metal and glass. "It *is* a piece of crap."

"So why are you trying to take it?"

She sniffed, wrenched her arm, and pried herself free. He let her. He had a feeling she wasn't going anywhere.

She handed back the camera. Rubbed at her wrist where he'd held her. "I didn't know you collected junk."

"You hungry?" he asked casually, retrieving his coffee and taking a sip, never letting go of her eyes. (His own eyes were green, pale and vivid like the center of a cut lime. They were mesmerizing, and he knew it.)

The girl didn't look away. "Yeah," she admitted. "I'm hungry."

"Then you could've just asked."

"Okay, do you have any money?"

"You can't eat money," he informed her. "What's your name?"

"Which one do you want?"

"The one you like best. Tell me your name, and I'll give you something to eat."

Her eyes narrowed. This sounded too much like something she'd heard before. "That's all you want?"

He didn't laugh at her. Not quite. He knew how the world worked, and it was a shame that she knew it too, at such a tender age. "Yeah, that's all I want. Don't worry, princess. You're not my type."

"Should I be offended?"

"No," he told her. "You should be a guy, if you want that kind of attention out of me."

She was new to the streets, obviously. Her clothes were dirty, but fairly nice. They'd been wet, and had dried with deep-set creases. Her jacket was still damp around the seams, where it hadn't dried out all the way. She was running from something, but whatever it was, the race had only just begun.

He idly thought he'd bring her in and get her story. Pioneer Square was no place for a kid, and certainly no place for a pretty piece of jailbait with all the street skills of peanut butter. If nothing else, he could give her a blanket to crash on and a meal, and see what he could find online. Someone was probably missing her, and that was bad. Or no one was missing her at all, and that was worse. Either way, he'd find out.

She opened her mouth to say something, maybe make a solid reply. Maybe offer him the truth instead of some snarky quip. But she didn't. She'd pulled her gaze away from his eyes, and once unlocked, she saw something else — something past him, something that horrified her to her very core.

She whispered, so softly that if he'd been another inch away he wouldn't have heard her: "Please don't chase me. He'll see."

She turned. She ran.

And Jackdaw didn't chase her. He didn't even look immediately over his shoulder to see what had scared her so badly. No, he took another sip of coffee and slipped his eyes to the right, as far as they could spy without turning his head.

He saw tourists and costumed guides, a street sweeper on the far side of First Avenue, pigeons wading in dirty puddles, cars jostling for parking, shoppers juggling their boutique bags and cell phones. Nothing at all to frighten him, or anybody.

But there was one man, standing alone, scanning the scene with far less discretion than Jackdaw. He was fortysomething and bland — so bland he might've been a plainclothes detective, or that was what sprung to mind. He was holding a small stack of papers, each sheet swathed in a clear plastic envelope to protect it from the rain.

Jackdaw watched as the man gave up his survey of the premises, selected one sheet, and pulled a staple gun out of his coat pocket. He affixed the plastic-clad notice to the nearest power pole, gave the scene one more glance, and headed off for the next block.

When he was good and gone, Jackdaw moseyed over to check out the posting.

MISSING: ANNE COOPER

RAN AWAY SEPTEMBER 28
REWARD

LAST SEEN WEARING JEANS AND A GRAY SWEATER, MAY HAVE BLACK CORDUROY JACKET. FOURTEEN YEARS OLD. VERY LONG BLACK HAIR. HALF CAUCASIAN, HALF ASIAN. ANNE MAY BE DISORIENTED AND CONFUSED. SHE IS IN NEED OF MEDICATION. IF YOU SEE HER, PLEASE CALL (206) 555-2080.

"Sounds like a lost dog," Jackdaw muttered to himself.

There was no picture, which was a little weird; and with only the text to go on, he wouldn't have sworn it was the girl who'd just tried to rip him off. But besides the long hair, the description was dead-on, and she sure as hell hadn't been confused. She'd been terrified.

He finished the last of his coffee and tossed the cup into the nearest recycling bin.

The girl was gone, vanished as thoroughly as a ghost. But this was Jackdaw's kingdom, and there were only so many places for a frightened newcomer to hide. By nightfall, he'd checked most of them. By dawn, he'd checked them all, and spotted her huddled on a third-floor fire escape that probably wouldn't have held the both of them.

He looked up at her huddled shape, half-hidden by a windbreaking wall made of cardboard, and he knew she was smart. Everyone looks down for things that are hidden. Everyone looks in holes, in drawers, in trunks, and in basements. That's why the best place to hide is up high — even if it's in plain view.

Nobody ever looks up, except people who've done a lot of hiding of their own.

TWENTY

"How far is it to the train station from here?" Trick asked, looking up at the sky as if he could find the sun and it might tell him what direction to look.

"As the jackdaw flies?" May almost laughed at her own joke. "A few miles. Maybe. It's all downhill from here, though. We could probably hoof it in an hour or two."

"I'm not chasing you again."

"Then we'll take the bus. Whichever one heads down Olive Street," she tried.

"You got any cash?"

"Enough to ride."

"Good." He nodded. His face was hard; he tightened the strap on his bag, and shifted it so it sat across his back. "Then let's go."

They didn't run to Olive Street, but they kept a cautious hurry. Two kids were running from an SUV on the news. Two kids matching their descriptions could lift any informed eyebrow. Couldn't they? Wouldn't they? May didn't know, but she forced herself to behave calmly as she took long strides, one foot after another, past the old houses and flat-faced condos, small square lawns, random offices and businesses, and the occasional Starbucks.

A bus was headed toward them, slowing down to make its stop beside the blue-and-white sign, so their timing was good for once. They hopped aboard and sat down in the back, on the seats that faced the center aisle. Never before had May wished quite so hard for a hoodie, or even a hat. She settled for her battered Walgreens sunglasses, dredged from the depths of her messenger bag. Trick popped in a pair of ear-buds and stared down at his phone, but the buds weren't plugged in to anything. May pulled out her own phone and pretended to flip through Twitter. Anything that let her keep her face down, with her hair falling forward.

Just thinking about talking to the cops made May sweaty and flushed, even as her hands were still cold and pale, her knuckles white as wax. What could she tell them? Nothing. Deny everything. Swear she had no idea why the madman in the SUV wanted to turn them into road pizza. He could've been chasing anyone.

No. She was already working on a story, and that couldn't be good. She was a decent storyteller, but a crap liar, for all the sense that made. Trick might be able to come up with something better. She looked at him sideways, watching him through a rumpled curtain of hair. His eyes were closed and his shoulders were hunched; he'd slipped down so low in the seat that she looked taller than him. His hair was fluffed up like May's, victim to the damp air and all the not-exactly-running through the old Hill's neighborhoods.

He looked young. But even slouched and feigning apathy, he looked a little bit fierce.

May hoped she looked fierce too. She crossed her arms and narrowed her eyes until they were almost shut, just a small sliver of eyeball squinting out angrily at the world. *Fake it till you make it,* she thought.

On second thought, that would probably be exhausting, because heaven only knew how long it'd take her to "make it." But she could fake it for the next day or two. She could hold it together long enough to reach Libby, and nothing else mattered.

Three years, that's how long she'd been dead.

Supposedly.

For May, it'd been three years of moving around, and bouncing back and forth between her parents . . . of making new friends, but not any good ones. It'd been three years of having a locker all to herself, and wishing it were different. But not anymore, because Libby was alive — and soon, everything was going to be okay again.

Nothing on earth could've convinced May otherwise, not even knowing that three years would change people, under the best of circumstances. May's three years had been boring and restless and inconsistent, but Libby's had been some kind of awful. It didn't matter, though. She had *survived*, just like in May's old dream about the car underwater and Libby kicking free, swimming up, swimming out. Escaping into captivity, and then escaping that too. Libby was definitely still Libby, wherever she was, whatever she was doing. She'd found allies like Jackdaw, and she'd stayed one step ahead of Ken Mullins for all this time. Of course she had. Because she was amazing, same as always.

Not three years and not thirty years would've changed that.

The bus turned left down by the market and followed the Sound for another few blocks. Then it redirected itself up a shockingly sharp hill and stopped, its last pause before starting the whole route over again. May and Trick exited quietly through the rear door, hopped onto the steep sidewalk, and headed toward Pioneer Square — and the train station that sat between it and the water.

May scanned the streets around them. She was hoping for some sign of Jackdaw. He could be anywhere. Any of these windows. Any of these doorways that didn't lead to storefronts but to walkups.

Libby could be behind any one of them too.

Trick was likewise keeping his eyes open; but without sunglasses, he was way too obvious. He looked nervous and wary, like someone who'd either just committed a crime or was about to. May elbowed him gently. "Play it cool, dude."

"I *am* playing it cool."

"Not very," she argued. She kept her head up, pretending to stare straight ahead. "Hey, watch out for those tourists."

He ducked away from a big clot of out-of-towners who were clustered together for the Seattle Underground Tour. When he stepped down off the curb, his boot startled a pigeon and rustled up something gross, but they kept going. They got honked at by a driver who apparently didn't know you were supposed to yield to pedestrians, and Trick flipped him off. "We're not very good at staying low-key or inconspicuous," he observed.

May took his hand and pulled him back onto the sidewalk, and then into Occidental Park. Another block and around a corner, and the streets came together in an enormous V-shaped interchange.

There it was: King Street Station.

The station was stately and grand, built from last century's brick and stone, with oversize windows, classic lines, and a great clock tower that scraped the ever-present clouds. On the street before it, lanes of jostling traffic competed for a spot at the stoplight, fought for the right to turn, and generally polluted the scene with a whole lot of noise and confusion.

"Do you see him?" May asked.

"No, and you're the one with the super-secret spy glasses."

"They aren't helping," she murmured, adjusting them. "But the message said 'King Street Station.' Let's go inside."

Trick sighed. "Sure, why not? Worst-case scenario, it was all a ruse, and it's really Ken waiting to murder us to death."

"At the station? In front of God and everybody? I doubt it," she said, but she didn't doubt it as much as she wished she did. "If he wanted to hurt us, he'd lure us someplace dark and quiet. Right?"

"Right. Just like he did in Fremont."

Past the little park they went, through the crosswalk, down an almost infinite number of concrete stairs, and into the great old station — its shiny floors and brass fixtures showing off its style instead of its age. The wooden benches gleamed, the ceilings were sky-high and covered in vintage tiles, and the station workers all wore crisp uniforms that stopped just short of looking corny.

But the place was bustling only a little bit. Perhaps thirty people waited for whatever train came next, and only half a dozen employees manned the ticket counters and baggage claim. In May's considered opinion, it was not as reassuringly crowded as the street outside.

Together, she and Trick sauntered through the place, though their saunter was more like an anxious stroll. But surely, Jackdaw wouldn't hold their uncoolness against them, May thought, and he would take them under his wing or whatever, and lead them right to Libby.

First she hoped, and then she *knew*. She took off her sunglasses, just to be sure.

"It's him," she whispered, almost to herself.

She nodded toward the back corner where a large display showed before-and-after shots of the station's renovation. There were pictures and maps, diagrams and letters. And there was a tall, thin guy a few years older than her.

He was still wearing all black, wrapped up tight in a long-sleeved shirt and skinny jeans that were crisscrossed with holes, showing ghost-white skin underneath. He wore sunglasses, like May, but his were black aviators — not the sales-rack special.

He didn't acknowledge them in any way. He just faced them, those bug-black lenses luring them across the immense, echoing space like a tractor beam. May took Trick by the arm and drew him along. Trick's eyes were wide and his knees were stiff, but he couldn't be that scared, could he? What was there to be afraid of? This wasn't the guy in the SUV; this was some punk who knew all about Libby, and who'd never done anything but help them. Maybe he wasn't scared, just nervous. Well, May was nervous too.

When she was close enough — when she could almost see him breathing, almost hear him idly tapping one foot — she said his name in a whisper: "Jackdaw?"

He nodded. Barely. A quick duck of his head. Trick just stood there — held in place by May's grip, or that's how it felt to her.

"It's you," May said. "I know it's you."

"You'd better hope so," he said. "There are worse things than birds watching the station."

"The Needle Man?" she tried. Were they talking in code? Perhaps.

But all they had in common was this story, and if the story held all the signs, all the words, then that's what she'd use.

"He's never far behind. And now he knows who you are, so you have two choices: You can stand still and let him catch you, or you can run."

Trick finally found his voice. "With you, I assume?"

"He hasn't caught me yet, and he's been chasing *me* longer than the pair of you. Besides . . ." He smiled down at May and tilted his head ever so slightly, and he said the only thing she wanted to hear in the whole wide world:

"The princess has asked to see you."

TWENTY-ONE

May's chest felt so tight she could hardly breathe. "So it's true. It's all true, and she's really *here*."

"She's nearby." Jackdaw looked up, scanning the scene. The crowd was growing, more people coming in the door.

"Then take me to her." May tried to make it sound like a command, like she wasn't begging, but it mostly sounded like she was praying.

"Right this way." He murmured the instructions softly, barely louder than a sigh, then unfolded his arms and turned on one heel. He walked like a bird flies, legs pumping like wings, feet barely grazing the polished floors. May and Trick hustled to keep in his wake. May had the awful feeling that if they lost him, he'd never come back for them — like if they couldn't keep up, they didn't deserve to come along.

Back through the train station they wound, between columns, down corridors, and past signs that said EMPLOYEES ONLY. But they never saw any employees, and no one ever stopped them.

"Down here," Jackdaw said without looking back. He opened a door that claimed to be an emergency exit. It also claimed that an alarm would sound, should anyone dare to open it. "I disabled it months ago," he said, still without looking at them, and slipped through into a stairwell.

The stairwell didn't look or feel like the rest of the station. It was cold, damp, and made of poured concrete from top to bottom, with boring metal handrails, and stains on the floors. There weren't any windows, and there wasn't much light. At every landing, a dim yellow bulb hung loosely from an old fixture that barely clung to the wall.

"What *is* this place?" Trick asked.

"It's a service corridor. Or it used to be, before the renovation," Jackdaw explained. "These days, there's a shorter passage between the maintenance areas and the engineer levels. When they did all that work a couple of years ago" — he ducked his head to avoid a dangling tangle of exposed wires — "they left a lot of empty spaces like this."

"So . . . do you come here often?" May tried, and it almost sounded like the joke it almost was.

"Often enough. It's the most direct way to the Underground, from this block."

Now he had Trick's attention. "We're going into the Underground? Won't we run into tourists?"

"Not where *we're* going."

The stairs bottomed out, and May figured they must be four or five floors beneath the surface. Behind this last flight was a stack of clutter: folding tables, janitorial equipment, chairs, broken ladders, and a bunch of other stuff she couldn't sort out in the dim, chilly light.

Jackdaw hopped down off the last stair and reached for the edge of a desk. It was lying on its side, and when he pulled it, it swung away smoothly, without the scrape and drag she expected to hear, revealing stairs descending into a dark tunnel below.

"Casters," he explained, pointing at a pair of tiny wheels she would never have noticed. "This is one of the back doors. Come on down, and watch your step. We don't have tourists, but there are plenty of rats to go around when you're this close to the water."

"Oh God," Trick said, and something about his queasy tone made May wonder if he had some specific and previously unmentioned fear of rodents. "But they're more afraid of us than we are of them. Right?"

"Not these rats, Hat Trick."

May frowned. "What did you call him?"

But their guide was already behind the desk, waving his ghostly hand for them to follow. In the dark beyond the stairwell, the sway of his long, thin fingers was all she could see.

She turned to Trick instead. "What did he call you?"

"My name, I guess," he muttered. "So is it still ladies first, or do you want to mix it up?"

"I'm going, I'm going." She crouched down low and shimmied behind the desk, into the dark below the city's underbelly.

Jackdaw waited for her there, in that in-between space left over from the city's engineering project more than a century ago. These were the rabbit warrens that connected Victorian era basements, shops, and stores — underground roads and thoroughfares all but forgotten once Seattle was lifted off the mudflats. May had only ever seen the main hub down by Pioneer Square, where the Underground Tour went. Those were the safe parts, wired for electricity and serviced by volunteer tour guides armed with trivia and laser pointers.

This was altogether different.

This volunteer tour guide stood slightly stooped to keep from hitting his head on a series of fat old pipes that ran along what passed for a ceiling. The sunglasses were gone now, and his face and hands were all she could see, until her eyes adjusted to the gloom. He was ghastly, unearthly. Neither smiling nor frowning, and scarcely moving at all as he waited for Trick.

Behind her, May heard her compatriot working up his courage and finding what footing was available. He slipped down behind her, into the grim, abandoned space, and the desktop door creaked shut behind him.

Jackdaw reached into a hole in the wall and retrieved a flashlight. When he flicked it on, the light was too much — only for a moment — and then it showed precisely what May would have expected: cobwebs, scuttling bugs, rusted metal, crumbling bricks, and a floor that wasn't even a floor. It was mostly dirt, with remnants of stones here and there. It was all wet, with standing puddles of stagnant water shining like mirrors.

Trick shuddered. "This is disgusting."

But Jackdaw disagreed. "No, it's only forgotten. There's plenty to appreciate about this place." He gestured for them to follow, and there wasn't much else May could do. When Jackdaw walked, he took the light with him, and everything else was the sharpest, most unforgiving dark she'd ever known.

Nervously, May chattered. "What do you appreciate about it? 'Cause right now, all I see is a good excuse for a tetanus shot."

He looked back, but the forward angle of the flashlight cast his face in funny shadows, outlining his cheek and nose with a thin beam of white. "I heard you had more imagination than that."

"Well . . . it's been a long day," she said weakly.

"For everyone, I expect." He resumed his progress, guiding them around the deepest puddles and under the lowest places where the ceiling drooped down to meet them. "But this is the perfect place for an adventure, don't you think?"

"The kind where the hero dies at the end," Trick muttered. He stepped into a particularly squishy spot of ground and grimaced.

"I should hope not," Jackdaw replied without looking at him. "Besides, if comics have taught us anything, it's that death is rarely a permanent condition."

"But we're not superheroes," May argued.

"Speak for yourself," Jackdaw told her. They drew up to a weathered-looking door that belonged on a porch someplace and not a thousand miles underground, wedged into the mud. "I'm prepared to live forever. And so is Princess X."

May felt that tight thrill again, that breathless squeeze in her chest, and she had to ask, because if she didn't, she wasn't sure she could keep following along in this dark, awful place. "Princess X . . . you know, don't you? You know that Libby and I made it up? You know she's the one who's drawing it, and it's been her all along."

"All along," he echoed. He reached for the door's knob and pulled, and another portal opened. There was light on the other side of this one, but not very much.

May grabbed his arm. "Wait. Please, just tell me. Just say it out loud. I need to hear it from someone else. *Please*, tell me she's alive."

He paused, then nodded as he gently pried her fingers away and let them go. "Of course she's alive. A good story never dies."

"That's not what I mean, and you know it."

"But we're almost there," he told her.

It still wasn't what she needed, but from pure desperation, she followed him anyway. And Trick followed her, and then the three of them were standing in a cleaner place, something more like an unfinished basement than a crawl space.

"We're almost *where*?" Trick asked.

"To the haunted house. Come on, it's only another block. She's waiting for you. Even though you haven't found all the keys yet."

"We were totally *going* to," May insisted. "And besides, all that's left was the last one — the gray child. That's Libby, isn't it? There you go. I found it."

The tone of his voice suggested he might be grinning when he replied, "Close enough."

On the wall was a small beige switch. He flipped it, and a humming chorus of fluorescent lights crackled on, weak at first and then stronger, steadier. The lights revealed a basement, or cellar, or something like that, packed from floor to ceiling with crates in one corner and old industrial machinery in another. Barrels, boxes, and the rusting corpse of a bicycle were scattered throughout, with a narrow path running through the clutter. The path was marked with footprints — some looked like they came from boots, others more like sneakers.

True to his word, Jackdaw brought them through one more subbasement and up one more flight of stairs. These were wood, and quite old. They squeaked, creaked, and sagged beneath their feet.

"Watch out for the broken one," he warned.

Trick said, "They all look broken."

"So watch out for *all* of them."

"This sucks, man. Get us out of here."

"I'm working on it, Hat Trick." Jackdaw flashed Trick a look of pure irritation. "I figured a kid with the guts to break laws like you would be a little more . . ." At the top of the stairs, one more door. He pulled out a key and unlocked it. "Intrepid."

May shot Trick a look too, but hers was all questions. Before she could ask, he said, "You already know I've done some . . . minorly illegal things to track down Ken."

"I don't think that's what he meant. And why does he keep calling you Hat Trick?"

Jackdaw didn't chime in either way. He opened the door, held it wide, and waved them both up the last few steps, offering enough distraction that Trick didn't have to answer. "Welcome to the haunted house," he said.

Trick said, "Wow," in a deliberately underwhelmed voice, but May gazed wide-eyed around the space, taking in the natural light pouring through a row of enormous windows, most of which were cracked or broken. Inside the oversize room was little else to remark, mostly discarded take-out containers, old wood shipping pallets, and an army of dust bunnies. It was not a place where people lived. It was a place people passed through.

"It's . . . it's lovely," she breathed anyway.

"Thank you," Jackdaw said graciously. "I'm rather fond of it."

"It's a mess."

"Shut up, dude." May aimed a light kick toward Trick's shin, but he dodged it. "It's neat."

"Its real name is the Starfish," Jackdaw supplied. "It used to be a hotel. Then it was . . ." — he waved one hand dismissively — "a number of other things. Now it's the headquarters of *All Free Peoples*, and a certain well-known webcomic called *Princess X*."

"You do it all from here?" Trick asked, skepticism dripping from his words.

"Not this floor, idiot. This is just for show. We like for people to see how abandoned and uninteresting it is."

"Well done. It's completely uninteresting."

Behind them, a patter of footsteps landed so softly that at first, May wasn't sure she'd heard anything at all. Or maybe she sensed it, tingling at the edge of her brain . . . some strange ESP sharpened in the last few days, the clues, the hunt, the danger.

The website.

The hairs on the back of her neck rose in anxious salute. She shivered, and turned around just in time to see the princess appear.

"Of *course* it's not interesting," she said. "That's why they call it plain sight, when you hide in it."

TWENTY-TWO

May froze.

The girl stood in a doorway at the entrance to another stairwell, which went up this time rather than down. . . . She was lean and pale, with hair that was shaggy and chin-length, cut shorter at some point, but growing out from a bad dye job that tried to be blond and was mostly orange. The roots were dark as chocolate, and dark as the fingerless gloves and the moth-eaten hoodie she wore, with a faded corporate logo that hovered above her heart. She wore knockoff Doc Martens that might've been real army boots foraged from Goodwill. They'd seen a lot of climbing, a lot of running.

The girl's smile was crooked and uncertain. And familiar.

"I knew you'd come, once you saw the site," Libby said. "I knew you'd find me."

Her voice was lower than May remembered, but it was steady and strong. Stronger than May's, which barely squeaked out her name — before she ran forward and flung her arms around the girl, squeezing harder, tighter, more fiercely than she'd ever squeezed anyone or anything before in her life. Not even when she rode her first roller coaster, and she'd clung to her dad like a barnacle. Not even when she fell off the pier before she could swim, and a man with a sailboat had thrown her a lifesaver.

She hugged Libby even harder than that, because sometimes, once in a while, her eyes would deceive her. But her arms had never lied to her yet, and here was Libby after all — warm and thin, and not so much taller than May anymore. Almost exactly the same height, and that was weird, wasn't it? In May's head, Libby was always impossibly tall, impossibly beautiful, impossibly young — immortal, even. But here she was, May's own age, returning the hug ounce for ounce, pound for pound.

"I didn't know what to do. I wasn't sure," Libby mumbled into May's shoulder. "I wanted to see you so bad, but I was afraid I'd get you killed."

"It's you," May finally gasped, still not letting go. Tasting that bleached-out hair, smelling sweat, stale coffee, and the faint odor of cigarettes smoked by somebody else. She wasn't sure she could look at Libby without crying.

"It's me," Libby agreed, nodding, hiding her own face in May's hair.

May said, "I'm so sorry."

"For what?" Libby asked, the question just as muffled as May's apology.

"For being a slow reader. For taking so long."

"Nah," she said, and finally drew back. She held May at arm's length. "You did great, once you started looking. Oh my God, look at you!" she exclaimed, her smile no longer crooked but wide, and happy instead of anxious. "You got tall!"

"You got short! And blond!"

"Yeah," she said, giving her head a self-conscious shake. "Not my idea. It was a bad disguise, that's all." She let go of May's shoulders, and the smile wavered but held.

Jackdaw chimed in. "I keep telling her to shave it. Bald is an even better disguise."

"But it's also something that makes people stare at you," Libby said, "especially when you're a girl."

"Maybe just a buzz cut. Nice and butch," May teased, reaching out to touch Libby's hair. "It doesn't matter. You're gorgeous, just like always."

"Oh, shut up," she said, almost blushing. "You're the gorgeous one now. You grew up nice, May."

May shivered to hear her name, and couldn't stop herself — she grabbed Libby again in another full-body hug. "No, *you* shut up. You're the princess, Libs. Always. Forever. God, I missed you so *much*."

"I missed you too." She hesitated, and gave the side of May's head a big, friendly smooch. "You really have no idea. When I started putting the comic together, God! I wished —"

Trick cleared his throat. "Ladies, I hate to interrupt this touching reunion, but there's still the matter of a maniac trying to kill us."

Libby let go of May and looked Trick up and down. "So *you're* the Hat Trick. I expected someone . . . taller."

"I get a lot of that," he said, with no small measure of irritation.

"Hat Trick. There it is again. Why does everyone call him that?" May asked. "It's just *Trick*."

Before Trick could weasel an explanation, Jackdaw supplied: "He's Patrick on his birth certificate, Trick in person, and Hat Trick on the Internet."

"You . . . you know each other online?" she guessed.

"We've met," Trick said tightly. "Digitally speaking."

Jackdaw did a little mock hat-tip and added, "There's more to this kid than you know."

"All good, I hope," she said nervously.

"Not all good, but not as bad as it might be. I was worried at first, because he was asking about the reward."

"There was a reward? Oh yeah . . ." May remembered. "He told me about it. How creepy."

Trick held up his hands. "I just remembered seeing it, that's all. I was trying to find the old 4chan and darknet posts about it. I was *investigating*, not bounty hunting."

May gave him a hint of stink-eye anyway. "Are you sure?"

"One hundred percent. Look, I never made contact with Mullins — just *him*." He jerked his thumb toward Jackdaw. "And in the end, it all worked out, right?"

It might've gone further and May might've asked more questions, but Libby cut off the interrogation before it could get under way. "You can sort it out later. For now, Jack . . . why don't you take Trick up to the second floor and show him your setup? You two can converse in your native computerese or whatever." They both looked at her like she was nuts, but she begged him, "Please? Can you guys give us a few minutes?"

Jackdaw sighed heavily and looked at Trick like he'd just as soon push him off a pier as take him upstairs. Trick didn't look much happier about the situation. "I promise not to touch anything," he vowed.

"All right, fine." Jackdaw pointed a finger gun at Libby. "Next coffee run's on you, though." He shook his head and said to Trick, "Stairs are this way."

When they were gone, Team Libby and May stood reunited. Libby said, "I'd offer you some hot chocolate, but I think we're out. And what we keep on hand isn't as good as Black Tazza's anyway."

"They tore it down, you know?"

"I only just heard about it, yeah. That was close! I mean, you following the clues and picking up the mask before they bulldozed the whole block. It would've been a huge pain to think of something new."

"We've always had great timing." May beamed.

"*You* always had great timing. I was always jumping the gun."

"Then we traded places, or that's what Trick would say. He accuses me of jumping to conclusions, but hey, it got me here!"

"Yes, it did! Oh, hey . . ." Libby said, looking over her shoulder. "We've got a mini-fridge over there. Want a Coke?"

"Yes!" May didn't need one, and didn't really care. But she wouldn't turn one down.

Around the corner was a kitchen-type area, or at least a spot with a small fridge and some cupboards full of food. Most of it was the boxed kind like Hostess cakes or chips, but some of it was hippie stuff like puffed vegetable sticks and dried kale.

"Help yourself to anything you see," Libby offered, retrieving the Cokes and gesturing at a long, dirty couch against the wall. "And don't fear the man-eating couch. It's old but it's clean, and it's crazy comfortable."

"That's why you call it a man-eater?"

"Uh-huh. You fall asleep on that thing, you'll never escape it."

They plopped themselves down on it, sitting cross-legged so close that their knees knocked together. Upstairs, May could hear footsteps creaking back and forth, and the low murmur of Jackdaw and Trick making awkward (but undoubtedly nerdy) conversation.

"I have to ask," Libby said suddenly, as though she'd only just remembered it. "Did you leave the tablet? And everything on it? Jack said you were going to put it in Christina's crypt."

"Yup." She nodded. "We stashed it there like he told us, and put the cover back on. Should we text my dad, or call the cops about it?"

"Yeah, we can call the nonemergency line and leave them an anonymous tip."

"But why, Libs . . . why didn't you just take the tablet to the police? Or send them the information on it, or something? Why didn't you just call me or email me ages ago? I would've come out here for you — I would've found a way, I swear!"

Libby looked like she was maybe going to cry. She wiped her nose with the back of her arm. "I *tried* going to the police — that's the first thing I did when I got away. But you-know-who had already filed a missing persons report on me, so they called him. He told them I was dangerous, that I was schizophrenic and I needed to be medicated, and that they shouldn't believe anything I said."

"Just like in the comic. I was afraid it was something like that."

"I was so freaked out, it didn't even cross my mind that he would've called the cops before I could get there — but that's what happened, and they believed him. So they tried to keep me there until he could collect me. It was going to take a few hours because he had to catch the ferry and everything, so they decided to move me to a psych ward for evaluation. But I kicked the orderly in the junk and jumped out of the van before it could leave the parking lot. Um . . . that's the short version," she concluded uncomfortably, as if the whole thing kind of embarrassed her. "So the next thing I did . . ." Her voice caught in her throat.

"You called your dad," May whispered. "We figured it out from the comics, and Trick looked it up. Ken killed him because he tried to come get you."

Libby nodded, then she set the can of soda aside and picked up May's hand, just to hold it. Quietly, she said, "My dad caught the first flight out. Booked it with his own name and everything, and same with the rental car. But ol' Needles, you know . . . he's such a tech head, it was easy for him to track down Dad before he could meet me." Her eyes were wet, but she still didn't cry. "After that . . . I was afraid to ask anybody for help. If he could sway the police, if he could track down my dad and kill him, then he could do anything to anyone. And maybe I wasn't quite right in the head, after all that time. . . ." She looked away. "I went downtown and I lived on the streets, because what else could I do? I didn't want to get anyone else killed. But I had never told him about *you*, and I never told him about Princess X, either."

"That's why you did the comic? To get my attention without getting Ken's? That's brilliant, Libs."

Libby didn't entirely agree. "Well, I did it for me too. It was kind of like therapy, maybe, telling the story, and drawing again. It gave me power." She was quiet for a moment. "Then Jack suggested posting it online to see if we could find you, and that sounded like a good idea at the time — but Needles caught on. Maybe he just stumbled across it or something, I don't know. I guess he thought it would give him a fresh lead on where I'd gone, but it didn't, not really. He couldn't track the IP address, not with the Great Firewall of Jackdaw on my side."

"And your clues in the comic were pretty subtle, I have to admit."

"Of course they were subtle. They were for *you*." Libby squeezed her hand, and May squeezed back. "I needed for you to dig up the info on this guy and make the connections — because it didn't matter if *I* gave it to the police. As far as the law's concerned, I'm just another crazy runaway teenager with a cracked-out story to sell. It had to come from someone else, and if it came from you . . . I thought maybe it'd protect you too. Like maybe he'd think twice about gunning for you if he knew you had evidence on him."

May did an awkward little laugh. "Yeah, that part didn't work out so great. He came for me anyway. Not that it was your fault," she added fast. "That one's on Trick."

"That's what Jack said — that your friend wasn't bad, but he wasn't careful."

"That pretty well sums him up. In his defense, though . . . he *did* get me here eventually. Him and Jackdaw together, I guess. I just wish it hadn't taken so long." She sighed. "When I realized the comic had been running almost six whole months, and I'd never seen it before, or even heard of it . . . I felt so *stupid*."

"Nah, don't feel stupid. It was just a webcomic, in a whole Internet full of webcomics.

"So how'd you end up drawing it anyway? How did you get here?"

Libby took a deep breath, and let it out slowly. "He kept me for almost a year, shut up in that house of his on Bainbridge, stuck mostly in one room. He called me Christine. For the longest time, I thought I was going to go crazy. I stopped eating, mostly, and I thought maybe I'd just give up and die, because it was the only way out of that house. But then . . . then I had this dream about my mom. She was yelling at me, telling me I had to stay strong because I had to escape. Hey, do you believe in ghosts?"

"Sure," May agreed quickly, not sure if it was true or not but not caring either way.

"Or dream ghosts, I guess. Maybe she was just in my head, but the dream got me moving again. It made me mad. It made me determined to get away from him — but then I had to get away from the police, and then the people from the psych ward. I couldn't stop anyplace . . . I couldn't *rest* anyplace, and it's not like I had any money. Then one day I met Jack downtown. I tried to rob him," she said with a faint hint of a smile. "Now he looks out for me. I've been living here ever since."

"Is he . . . is he your boyfriend?"

"Boyfriend? No, but *he's* got one. Jack can't even think straight."

May was relieved to hear it — that Jackdaw didn't want something ugly in return for his help. She liked him, and she didn't want to think of him that way. "Does he make a habit of taking teenagers off the streets?"

"He's done it before, but it's usually druggies. He has a history with the addiction and recovery folks, so that's his soft spot. He also doesn't like cops, and the cops are pretty hard on the street kids around here, so sometimes he takes in other strays too." She paused and looked around at the space. "I think I've stuck around longer than anybody so far, but then again, it's not like I have anyplace else to go."

"We'll fix that," May declared.

Libby giggled at her.

"What? I totally mean it."

"I know. That's not what's funny: Your accent came back *hard*-core."

"Shut up! No, it didn't," May giggled back.

From the stairwell, they heard Jackdaw call, "You two aren't fighting already, are you?" And then he appeared, with Trick in tow.

"Speak of the devil," Libby said. "And I'm just teasing her, and she knows it."

"She can pick on my accent all she likes. But what about you two? Did you bond or anything? At least you didn't kill each other." May meant it to be silly, but they both looked grim, so she asked, "What's going on? What are you so upset about?"

"Ken's on the move." Trick pulled a small smartphone from his back jeans pocket and handed it to Libby. "He's no fool, so he's making a run for it."

"A run for what?" May asked.

Jackdaw shrugged. "He's probably headed home to Bainbridge, to fry his server farm and flee the country. He knows you can prove Libby's identity, or he's afraid you can; if nothing else, you can raise enough stink to exhume her grave. Besides that, he already knows Trick turned up Libby's test results from the bone marrow registry, because he stole that intel right off Ken's server. The connections have been made, and the noose is tightening. He'll want to get out while he can."

Trick frowned. "What I took from his server . . . wait, you mean the numbers in the mask? That PDF from the clinical drug trial? I thought the numbers were Ken's daughter's patient ID."

"No, they were about Libby — and it wasn't a drug trial. It was a registry drive sponsored by the drug company, and —"

May interrupted, "Libby never had cancer!"

"No, I never had it," Libby explained. "But back before you moved here, there was a kid in my class who did, and her parents were looking for a marrow match. Everyone in the school wanted to help out, so a lot of the students got tested. But nobody was a match, and she died. It was really sad."

Jackdaw picked up the tale. "The students were minors, so their results went into the donor database by case number, not name. All that information was sent back to the hospital." To May, he said, "That's how Ken discovered that Libby was a match for his daughter in the first place. He owns the private server farm where the hospital offloads their old records. He hid what he'd done by swapping the document titles with some related drug trials, just to bury his trail a little better. That's why it was under the Xerberox name."

May stood up and slapped her empty Coke can on the nearest counter. "Okay!" she said. "I think I understand everything. Or . . . I understand enough for now, I think, and finally we're all *here*. Libby's alive, and we can prove it. That's the important thing."

"No," Jackdaw contradicted her. "The important thing right this second is catching and stopping Ken."

Trick threw his hands up. "He could be home by now, and he might've already taken a flamethrower to the place."

Jackdaw answered, "But he's not. I know that because I put a tracker on the SUV after he ditched it in Fremont. I had a feeling he'd be back for it. He reported it stolen yesterday — always thinking ahead, that one — and once it cleared the impound, he went back to collect it."

"That was . . . gutsy," Trick said.

"In my experience," Jackdaw said, "rich white guys with expensive clothes and good manners usually get what they ask for."

Libby said, "He probably just walked right into the precinct, told them his car had been stolen, handed over a fake insurance card or his driver's license, and got it back in under an hour."

Trick cocked a thumb at Jackdaw. "But not before this guy bugged it?"

"I stuck the GPS under the back bumper before they had a chance to tow it." Checking the smartphone's screen, he added, "And he's headed . . . west."

Libby leaped to her feet. "We have to do *something*."

May suggested, "We can call the cops — they'll get to his house before we could. You know where he lives, right, Libby?"

"Call the cops?" Jackdaw asked with a sneer. "And tell them what? They don't believe Libby's who she says she is, and we'll never get there in time to convince them. They'd just let him go, if they even bothered to detain him. I guess we could say he's the Fremont maniac, but they gave him back his car. They obviously don't think he's a serious suspect."

"We could tell them he's got something evil stored on his servers," Trick tried. "A terrorist plot."

"I like the way you think, man, but it's risky — and here's why," Jackdaw told them, pulling up a chair. He turned it around and straddled it, leaning forward thoughtfully while he talked. "If we tell them that there's evidence of anything bad stashed on his little server farm, the cops will seize the whole shebang. So even *if* they don't screw up the machines and damage the data by accident, it'd be months, maybe years, before they sorted through it all and found the right file. And they'd turn him loose in the meantime."

Trick shook his head unhappily. "Yeah, you're right. Cops, feds, spooks . . . you name it, none of those guys are any good with sensitive equipment."

"Then what do we do?" May asked desperately. "We can't just teleport over to his house and swipe all his stuff before he gets there!"

The silence that fell in the wake of her silly suggestion did not make her feel any better.

Slowly and almost reluctantly, Jackdaw said, "Well . . . I mean, we don't need *all* his stuff . . . just a handful of incriminating files, you know — the stuff that matches up Libby and his daughter. Hell, if we're *really* lucky, there might be records of Libby's blood work, and even DNA from before she disappeared, and that would make her identity ironclad. It'd put him away for life."

Libby ran her fingers through her ratty hair. "Do you think we could beat him home?"

Jackdaw looked at the smartphone, with its flashing dot that marked Ken's SUV. "It's coming up on rush hour, and he'll probably have to wait a turn or two for the ferry. We won't, if we ride it on foot. Or we could always pursue . . . alternate means of getting there. Do you know where he keeps his server farm? It must be somewhere in that house."

"Not exactly," Libby said. "He mostly made me stay on the second floor, or in the attic. All the doors on the first floor were closed and locked all the time, and I don't know about the basement. The house is big, but it's not *that* big. And server farms are huge, aren't they?"

"If he's just doing some freelance hosting, it might fit in a single room. Most likely it's the basement, or behind one of those closed doors on the first floor. He'd have to keep it all someplace with good climate control, or it'd get too hot."

They were seriously thinking about invading Ken's house, May realized — seriously talking about it, and planning for it. This was crazy. Entirely crazy, and dangerous, and unlikely to boot. But May had come this far, solved this much, and there was no turning back now — even if she wanted to, not while this lunatic murderer was out there. None of them would ever be safe until he was stopped, Libby especially.

May couldn't stand the thought of it. Not when she'd only just now gotten her back. "Then let's do this, if it's the only good chance we'll get."

Trick's eyes were locked on May. "You know what? Screw that guy. I'm on board too."

"Are you sure? All of you?" Jackdaw looked hard at Libby. "Libby, do you really want to go back to that house?"

She looked halfway terrified and halfway ready to roll. "No, of course not. But I don't want him to get away, either."

Jackdaw's mouth was set in a sharp line, and his eyes were hard. He was thinking, calculating, already mentally preparing for whatever they were going to need — May could almost see the gears turning in his head, and it gave her hope, every bit as much as it scared her.

Having reached some conclusion, he said, "If I can get into his physical system, I can cherry-pick the important stuff and send it to the cloud, or put it on a drive. I know what we're looking for, and if I can just see his setup, I can grab what we need in less than a minute. I wish there was some way we could do it remotely, but there's not. Believe me, I've tried. We have to do this on-site."

"But, Jack . . ." Libby faltered. "I owe you so much already."

He grinned at her, warm but not weird. "Kid, you've been the craziest adventure of my life so far. I need to find out how this ends. Besides, we can't trust Junior here" — he popped a thumb toward Trick — "to go in the system and get away clean."

"Hey!" he objected, but Jackdaw patted him on the shoulder, as if to say he hadn't meant anything by it.

"Great," May said, despite the terrified hitch in her throat. "So . . . the fearsome foursome?" She shoved her right hand into the space between them all, and one by one, the others slapped hands down on top of hers.

"Okay, then," Jackdaw said. He pulled his hand out of the pile and checked the phone again. "It's settled. We make for the dock now, before Ken's SUV beats us to the ferry. We can do this, but we have to make a run for it."

TWENTY-THREE

They started in the Underground, ducking through basements, cellars, and the unfinished spaces that honeycombed beneath the streets of Seattle. A lot of the Underground was disappearing, Jackdaw told them as he guided them through it. "Property values have gotten so high, people want to use the space." He sidled through a cascading series of vertical pipes. "It costs a lot of money, but developers are still turning it all into offices or storage. Watch your step," he warned.

They emerged at another doorway that didn't have a door, but it had a step that dropped much lower than it ought to. The foundation had sunk away by a couple of feet, and the whole room looked like it was escaping slowly through an unseen hole in the floor.

"Where *are* we?" May asked. The answer wouldn't mean anything to her, but she felt so lost that she'd take any answer at all. Mostly, she wanted to hear that somebody knew what they were doing and where they were going. Jackdaw sometimes paused and pondered, and she wondered how well he really knew his way around this labyrinth under the city.

"We're close" was all he replied.

"That's not your most *specific* response ever," Libby said.

"Okay, then we're *really* close. The ferries are about a block away."

"So what about the SUV?" Trick wanted to know.

"Not enough signal down here to tell. I'll check again when we're topside. If he's heading to the ferry from the impound lot, we've got rush-hour traffic on our side. We'll beat him by twenty minutes, easy. I think."

May pulled out her phone and checked it, in case he was wrong. One single bar flickered off and on. Mostly off. "What if he's *not* headed to the ferry?"

Trick hopped off the step. "Where else would he go?" he said.

She put away the phone and jumped down. "I don't know. Our apartment building? He went after Libby's dad. . . . What if he makes a play for our parents again?"

Jackdaw turned the big flashlight on the pair of them. "Last I saw, the cops were all over that place. I wouldn't worry about it."

And Libby reminded them, "You saw the tracker. He was coming *this* way, not back up the hill."

Jackdaw led them to a flight of cracked cement stairs with an iron bar for a railing. It was slick and rusted, both dirty and damp. May tried not to touch it as she climbed.

When the door at the top opened, daylight the color of a latte spilled down onto the steps.

"Come on, hurry," Jackdaw said, drawing them out to a space just below street level. The sidewalk was only a few feet above them; they were nestled against the side of an old building, next to a city construction sign. "Don't let anyone see you. If they know we come and go from here, they'll close it up so we can't."

The four of them hastily piled onto the sidewalk and shoved their hands into their pockets, checked their phones, and adjusted their jackets or sweaters. May had never realized how hard it was to act normal.

"The signal's back," Libby murmured, pointing at the screen Jackdaw held for her to see. "But the SUV's not moving anymore. He's parked it or ditched it. Or else he's stuck in traffic."

"Where?" Trick asked.

She stared at the screen, using her palm to shield it from the glare. "Near the train station. He might've somehow chased you there, or maybe he just went that way because he thought the traffic would be better."

Jackdaw shrugged. "Then he obviously hasn't spent much time downtown. Anyway, if he's still with the vehicle, we have the lead."

"We'll lose it at the ferry if we don't catch the boats just right," May declared. "Oh God . . . what if we end up on the *same one*?"

Jackdaw agreed. "You're right, that would suck. So maybe we should do this another way — we could always make the trip on a Zodiac. It'd be a little rough, but we'd beat the ferry to the Bainbridge dock."

Trick was appalled. "A Zodiac? One of those little inflatables with a motor? We'd hit a seal, or a bird or something. We'd never make it all the way to the island that way."

"They're not *that* fragile, and they're really fast." May could see Jackdaw was warming to the idea, even as she found it more frightening by the moment. "We might have to dodge the Coast Guard, but that's not such a big deal."

"Do you even know *how* to get to Bainbridge Island from here?" she asked. "Do you have a map or something?"

"Don't need a map. I've done it before."

Libby turned to May. "If Jack says he's done it before, that means he remembers everything about it. He's a genius with spatial relations."

"I'm sure that means something awesome," May replied nervously. "But the idea of surfing across Puget Sound in a big inner tube isn't my idea of a good time."

"Mine either," Libby admitted, dropping back to take her arm in a halfway hug. "But we're not doing this for a good time, and it could be worse. I could be doing it alone again. In a rowboat."

May leaned into the hug, drawing strength from the strong, solid presence of Libby — who was not a ghost, and never had been. She was the princess with a purple katana sword instead, the avenging gray child. She said into her old friend's ear, so softly that the boys didn't hear it, "I trust you."

And Libby squeezed her in reply. "*Good.*"

May's phone vibrated in her pocket, but when she checked, it was just her dad again. She put it away. He didn't need to know what they were doing.

Unless he *did.*

Maybe *someone* ought to know, just in case this didn't pan out . . . in case they were washed away in the Zodiac, tossed into the Sound, and left to sink or swim. In case they didn't beat Ken Mullins home.

"Guys, how about this . . ." May offered, as they drew up to a tiny shop down by Alaskan Way. "Jackdaw, you said you could swipe the information you need in less than a minute. So what if we call the cops once we get to Ken's house? It'll take them a lot longer than a minute to get there, but if we can't get away clean, we might need backup. He might catch us, and he's killed people before."

Libby nodded. "I know you don't like cops, but for real" — she put a hand on Jackdaw's arm — "we need him dead or in jail, and I'm probably a crappy murderer."

"All right. Just this once, we can give them a heads-up. One of us can pull a 911 once we're inside, and that'll give me plenty of time. Does that make you happy, May?"

"Happier, I guess."

"I'll take it. And for now, you guys stay out here. I'll be right back." Jackdaw poked his head into a tiny tattoo shop and exchanged a few words with a heavily pierced kid in a Mohawk.

While the others milled about, May took out her phone and composed a text message for nobody but her dad to see. KEN MULLINS. BAINBRIDGE ISLAND. GO TO LAKE VIEW AND LOOK IN THE CRYPT WHERE THEY PUT CHRISTINA MULLINS. She read it and reread it, wondering what else she ought to say. By the time Jackdaw emerged with a set of keys, she figured it couldn't hurt to add, FOUND LIBBY.

But once they were loaded into a small black boat, knees knocking against each other, shoulders hunched against the wind blowing off the water, she hit SAVE. She couldn't send the text yet — or else her dad would call the cops, and the whole thing would be blown before they ever arrived. But just in case it all went south, and Ken caught them, and the cops never arrived in time . . . she could send that text and he'd know where to start looking for her.

Or for her killer, if it came to that. She shuddered and tucked the phone back into her pocket.

Nobody spoke as the borrowed Zodiac rumbled to life and scraped over the rocks, away from the spot where it had been tied for safekeeping.

Jackdaw manned the engine like he'd done it before, maybe a lot of times, so May tried not to worry about that part. They had plenty of gas — he'd made sure before they left. They could make it back to the city when they were finished, if they missed the last ferry back. If they didn't, Jackdaw said they could leave the Zodiac on Bainbridge for another friend to retrieve later on.

She looked up at the sky and tried to feel good about the sprawling orange light still keeping everything bright off to the west. Then she looked back at the city, its sparkling coastline and jagged buildings with their lights just now coming on . . . and she felt a little sick.

It might have been the motion of the Zodiac, bouncing up and down on the waves as they hurtled across the afternoon-dark water. It could've been the sight of the enormous ferry, still docked at the pier . . . and then, with a loud crow of its horn, slipping slowly away, following along in their tiny wake, the Needle Man probably on board.

Or it might have been the realization that nobody had a life vest, and that they were about to break and enter at a murderer's house.

Whatever it was, her stomach stayed light and nasty, sloshing around in her torso, even when Libby wrapped an arm around her. But Libby wasn't quite windbreak enough to keep the cool air from working into the nooks and crannies of May's corduroy jacket, and there wasn't enough juice in the Zodiac's motor to outrun the sunset. Dusk crept up behind them, nipping at their heels. It tagged along behind the bouncing boat, and nobody talked about it — because nobody talked about anything. This wasn't just an adventure, it was life or death. And what could you say about life or death?

These were the things she considered as she held on tight to Libby, so tight that she hardly noticed when Trick sat back on the low, narrow seat on her other side. If Libby minded Trick's presence, she didn't say anything about it. She just yelled into May's ear, to make herself heard over the motor and the wind: "We're almost there."

May could see the island, a low, green line approaching fast . . . but when she looked back over her shoulder, she saw the ferry looming up behind them. If Ken Mullins was on that ferry — and she had a dark, sour spot in her heart that said he *must* be — then their lead was shrinking.

Jackdaw guided the Zodiac under the pier, letting the motor drop to a quiet hum. It still felt loud in May's ears; it left a little buzzing noise where the silence ought to be. But she could now hear the grumpy seabirds overhead, settling down for the night, and she still felt the chilly, anxious thud of Libby's heart until she untangled herself.

The Zodiac stopped.

A rope was coiled in the bottom of the boat, and May handed it up to Jackdaw when he asked her for it. He tied them off to a post, very near to the slippery rocks that still stood above the water. The tide would change that, in another few hours — but with any luck, they'd be gone much sooner.

"Everybody out," Jackdaw ordered, keeping his voice low and careful. "There's a ladder up ahead, just over those rocks. Watch your step."

"You really *have* done this before?" May asked him.

"I used to come this way every now and again," he said, helping them one by one up the rocks, and then pointing the way to the ladder.

It was almost too dark to see Jackdaw now, especially since he was wearing all that black. But they couldn't rely on the flashlights, not when the ferry was blowing its whistle, warning the pier that it was coming home to roost, and telling everyone to get ready.

Libby paused at the bottom of the ladder. "This is where . . . no, come to think of it. It was over there . . ." She cocked her head a bit to the south.

"Where you what? Where you escaped?" May asked.

If there was a spell, or a moment, it broke as soon as it happened. Libby shook it off. "I don't know. It was around here someplace. It was dark and raining. It was a long time ago."

Up the ladder they went, one by one, single file, into the dim, creaking docks that held small dinghies and another Zodiac or two.

"Okay, Libby," May said, staring back and forth between the arriving ferry and the darkness on the other side of the pier. "Which way?"

Libby set off walking. "Follow me."

"You remember exactly?" Trick asked her. "I mean, *exactly* exactly? Because it's really damn dark, once you get away from the pier."

"It was really damn dark when I got away from the house," she reminded him. "All I have to do now is backtrack. It's pretty much a straight shot — past the main drag, and up that hill."

May didn't see whatever hill Libby meant, but she trusted her, just like she promised. "Should we turn on the flashlight?"

"Wait until we're farther away from the road."

"But I can't see a thing," Trick complained.

Jackdaw agreed with him. He dug the light out of his backpack, turned it on, and partly shielded it with his hand. "It's cool, I've got it. We'll break our ankles out here if we can't see."

When they were far enough off the beaten path that Libby deemed it safe, she commandeered control of the light. May fell back beside Trick in the lineup, with Jackdaw bringing up the rear. After a few seconds, their eyes adjusted to the scene. They were at the edge of a neighborhood with a sign that said GLENWOOD PARK. A pair of street lamps flanked the sign, giving the sidewalk a golden glow.

Libby told them, "Ken's place is two streets up. It's a big yellow house with square white columns."

Jackdaw said, "Everybody, keep your eyes open for cars or other people. There's always the chance we've been wrong and he's already home."

They made their way back into the neighborhood, up a hill.

Libby froze. She stared forward without even blinking.

And there was the house, and it was just as Libby had said: large, with squared-off columns as white as china. The rest was a shade of yellow that looked sickly in the distant lamplight. It made May think of her uncle's eyeballs, when he'd been in the hospital, with his kidney dialysis machine humming and buzzing. Something about the place felt sick, and angry, and hostile, just like the Needle Man's house in the webcomic.

May stood still beside her friend. After too many moments of too much quiet, she whispered, "Libs?"

"The living room light's on, but he always leaves a light on. He leaves the lights on, and all the curtains drawn," she added more quietly. "It's hiding in plain sight."

Jackdaw put a hand on her shoulder. "Are you sure you're up for this?"

"It doesn't matter," Libby said. May wondered if she really meant it, or if she only wanted to believe it. "Because it's us or him, and it's now or never." She wiped her sea spray–dampened hair out of her face and turned to her friends. "I choose him. And I choose *now*."

May murmured something that sounded like "me too." Then she turned away and quietly pulled her phone out of her pocket. She pulled up the text she'd composed to her dad and pressed SEND.

TWENTY-FOUR

They arranged a signal among them: If anyone saw anything that looked like Ken, inside or out, they'd text everyone the word *needles*. They synchronized their cell phones with one another's numbers, so they were as prepared as they were going to get.

May didn't like checking her phone, though. She didn't like seeing how many times her dad had tried to reach her (eleven), or how even her mother was calling from Atlanta now (three times). She didn't recognize some of the other recent numbers, but assumed they were law enforcement. Now, for safety's sake, she turned on the vibration but left off the volume. She jammed the phone into her back pocket.

May and Trick followed Libby and Jackdaw up to the house. The bushes were scratchy when she ducked between them, hugging the side of the house behind Libby, who acted with single-minded focus. May thought of the princess in the comic, and her sword. She thought of the quest, and the Four Keys, and how the time had come to set the princess and her whole kingdom free. They were writing the final chapter in real life. She wondered what the artwork would look like on IAmPrincessX.com, and the thought gave her a shaky smile.

They felt their way along the brick foundation and the wood slat siding, adjusting their path to dodge an air-conditioning unit — which surprised May a little, because she didn't know anyone in Washington ever bothered with one. From the corner of her eye, she saw Trick watching her. He was shivering a little. May put out a hand to touch his arm, pretending she was trying to keep in line and help them stay close together — when really she just wanted to touch somebody for reassurance. His uncertainty made her feel less silly, and less like a traitor, for having her own fears.

Every time they reached a window, Libby pressed her back against the house and crept up to it until she could turn her head and see inside at an angle. The curtains were all pulled shut, but they didn't offer perfect coverage — and over by the kitchen window, they were high and sheer.

Libby crouched back down beside them. "I'm pretty sure he's not home."

"So how do we get inside?" May asked.

"See that next window? The lock's broken. Once upon a time, I'd planned to escape that way, but that's not how it worked out. I bet he doesn't know about it. I bet he never fixed it."

"Is it big enough for us to fit through?"

"Sure," she said, looking Trick up and down. "*He's* barely any bigger than we are."

"Thanks," Trick said.

"It was an observation, not an insult. And Jack's tall, yeah — but he's skinny enough to worm inside. I'll go first, make sure the coast is clear, and then you guys can come in behind me."

"What are we looking for?" May asked. "The servers, I know, but I'm not even sure what a server looks like."

"*I* know," Jackdaw said, "so you shouldn't worry about it." Then he added, "It's basically just stacks of computer equipment. If for some reason I can't chase it down, and you find a room full of machines with flickering lights, let me know so I can plug myself in. Even if the cops don't catch him at anything, even if he slides through the net this time, he'll never know I got inside his data. I won't trip any alarms with an IP, like Baby Einstein over here."

"Hey!" Trick objected.

"You two knock it off, would you?" Libby reached up and found the sill, and gave the window's frame a small wiggle. It creaked and squeaked, but held firm.

May said, "Trick, give her your pocketknife."

"Multitool," he grumbled, but obliged — and Libby went to work with the screwdriver blade. In twenty seconds, the window gave way with a tiny crack. It sounded like fireworks in the otherwise quiet night. They all held still, waiting for the anxious moment to pass; and when it did, Libby shoved the window up. It scooted jerkily open, its old glass and old frame swollen with the ocean air, and when May stood up to see it, she saw that it had been almost painted shut. Unlocked or no, it was a miracle that it opened at all.

Libby handed the multitool down to May, who slipped it into her jeans pocket without thinking about it. Jackdaw pulled himself up to the windowsill with his hands, and with a little jump he slipped inside, smooth as an eel. He spent five or ten seconds investigating, then put his head through the window and declared, "I don't hear anything. Come on."

He reached his hand through the window, and Libby took it. She was already pulling herself up onto the ledge when May got down on one knee and offered it as a stepping-stone. Libby agreed to the assistance, and with Jackdaw's help as well, she wiggled headfirst through the window.

Inside, she said, "I'm fine, Jack. Get hunting." Then she called, "All right, May. Your turn."

Trick said, "Go ahead. I'm right behind you."

May slithered through the opening and let Libby catch her on the other side. She stood up in a tiny, old-fashioned bathroom, with white subway tiles and tiny black-checked patterns on the floor, and thirty seconds later, Trick stood beside them too.

Libby put one hand on May's shoulder and one on Trick's. "Stay away from windows, or stay low when you pass in front of them. Don't turn on any extra lights, either. He'll notice it from the street."

Trick shivered. "You've given this a lot of thought."

"I had a lot of time to think," she said, and looked both ways into the hall. "Trick, you call the cops. Tell them we're at 3502 Willow Heights. I'm heading upstairs to see if there's anything useful in his bedroom, maybe more servers, or hard drives, or anything like that.

Then I'll come back downstairs and join you, and we can poke around the first floor. Jack'll probably have found the server room by then."

"Got it," May and Trick said.

Libby dashed out of the bathroom to the end of the hall, and up the flight of stairs at the far landing. May and Trick hesitated a moment behind her, then Trick started to dial and May bolted.

She wound up in the living room, not that she really knew what she was doing there. Should she look for the servers? Evidence of Libby's captivity? Would she even know it, if she found something?

She stood in the center of the room, then remembered she was supposed to steer clear of the windows — and a big pair of long curtains were the only thing separating her from being seen from the front yard. She ducked away and started rifling through an end table's drawer, which turned out to hold a TV remote and some old magazines, but nothing else of interest.

It all felt very invasive and weird. She didn't like looking through other people's stuff, even if those other people in question were creepy murderers. Her whole life, she'd been taught to respect other people's property . . . more or less . . . and this was exactly the opposite of that.

But Libby was storming around upstairs, and Trick had finished his phone call to the police; he was rooting around in the kitchen — yes, he was in the kitchen, she was pretty sure. She heard a drawer open, and silverware sliding and clattering.

At the back, she heard Jackdaw trying doors and either opening them or breaking them down.

Determined to carry her own weight in this burglary, she tried the other end table, but its sole drawer had nothing inside but dust bunnies. Next up, the bookcase. She pulled out fistfuls of volumes, shoved them aside, and found more dust with the added bonus of at least one good-size spider. Trespassing wasn't always everything it was cracked up to be.

Libby came thundering down the stairs. She and May nearly collided with Jackdaw on the first-floor landing.

"Did you find anything?" May asked him. Trick came out to join them.

"Nothing but old boxes and books. Libby, where's the basement?"

"Back over there." She pointed toward a solid-looking door that stood unobtrusively just inside the kitchen.

Outside, they heard the faint rumble of an engine. A slim seam of light caught the edge of the living room curtain and slipped across the room.

They looked back and forth at each other, eyes wide, everyone ready to panic and not quite panicking yet. "It's too soon to be the cops," May said.

"And there are no sirens," Jackdaw added.

"*Out*," Libby whispered, the single word loaded with three years of terror.

If Libby wanted to leave, that settled it — they were leaving. The girls tripped over each other, with Trick on their heels, and they all jostled together to reach the foot of the stairs.

Jackdaw dithered at the rear. Libby stopped when she saw he wasn't coming. "Jack, come on!" she begged, while May and Trick dashed toward the bathroom so they could escape back out that stupid little square window.

The lights slid brighter around the curtain seams. Headlights. They were turning into the driveway that led up to the house, and beside it. Right underneath that bathroom window.

Trick figured it out as soon as May did. They faced each other with matching expressions of horror, both wondering what they should do now that their secret exit was cut off. Jackdaw said quietly but forcefully: "Not that way. Downstairs, into the basement!"

"But we'll be trapped!" Trick squeaked.

May squeezed his upper arm, probably hard enough to hurt him through his jacket. "There might be another door down there, a cellar door or something. And the cops should be here soon, right? You called them, what . . . maybe two or three minutes ago? The island isn't that big. We won't have to hide for very long."

"Okay, downstairs." He wrenched himself free.

"Hurry up." Jackdaw ushered them back down the hall toward the closed door Libby had indicated. He yanked it open and drew them all inside, down into the very darkest place yet — underground, with nothing but a few slender windows to let in any light. If there was a chain for a bulb, they didn't dare pull it. Not while the car was parking, and the emergency brake was setting with a crunch, and the driver's door was opening, then shutting again with something too soft to call a slam.

Footsteps, long strides, rounded the house to the front door.

A key rattled in a lock.

Downstairs, they reached a poured concrete floor that echoed every step from corner to corner of the mostly empty space. But it also echoed the hum and buzz of a dozen tall servers, standing like sentinels in the chilly, dark room. Jackdaw pulled out his phone and used the glow of its face to illuminate the towers. The machines weren't quite the obelisks they appeared at first glance; they were stacked atop one another on twelve metal shelving units, looking for all the world like a graveyard for old desktop computer cases, except that they throbbed and chattered softly back and forth. Little lights flickered here and there.

"Retro setup," Trick breathed.

Jackdaw nodded and pulled up a flashlight app on his phone. "Old-fashioned, but effective."

Then they barely — but distinctly — heard the front door's lock unfasten upstairs, and the doorknob turn. No one moved except Jackdaw, who fished a flash drive out of his pocket and went patrolling the metal shelves, looking for the spot he wanted. May glanced around the basement. There was no cellar door.

She wondered what response the Needle Man would offer upon seeing that someone had invaded his lair. Drawers were opened everywhere, and doors that were supposed to be closed and locked weren't anymore.

At least one window was still ajar. She closed her eyes and listened hard. For thirty seconds, then forty-five, she heard nothing at all.

Then Ken began to walk, slowly and with great caution, around the first floor. His feet were as careful as a cat's, but the pressure on the boards above betrayed his presence. The four fugitives in the basement could plot his course as clearly as if they could see him.

May searched the darkness for Libby. Her eyes were adjusting, and she could see Libby's face now — her friend's eyes were huge and wet, and her mouth was tight with fear. "Jackdaw?" she whispered. "How's it coming?"

"Found it," he said in response, but May didn't know what that meant. He was fiddling with something small and plastic, and it sounded like perhaps he'd found a keyboard with very soft buttons. His body mostly blocked the dim glow of a small screen.

"How long do you need?" May wanted to know.

Jackdaw said, "A minute more . . . I'm trying to find Libby's blood-work and stuff."

"Just . . . hurry up, please?" Libby said quietly. "I want to get out of here."

May shook her head. "Maybe he'll go upstairs, and then we could make a run for it. Let's wait until we have a head start."

"Where are the cops?" Trick wondered aloud. "It's been five whole minutes."

"Shh!" Jackdaw warned.

May thought she was going to explode. She could practically *feel* the weight of the house overhead, and every step the Needle Man took reverberated like the old place had a heartbeat. "We have to get out of here!" Libby said in a weird half croak.

"He doesn't know we're still here," Trick said. "He'll head upstairs before long . . ."

As he said it, the timbre of the footsteps changed — and rose. They went from a stride to a climb, and May counted them without really meaning to.

"See?" Trick said. "Now we just have to slip out the front door, or back through the bathroom. Let's get ready to scatter. Jackdaw? Where are you at?"

After a brief pause, he replied, "*Finished.*" May heard the soft slide and click of a flash drive being removed.

"We can't really scatter," Libby murmured, following him. "That's a good idea, but there are only a couple of ways *out* . . . and the front door might be locked from the outside. It was always locked from the inside and the outside too. . . . Maybe if we had some kind of distraction . . . ?"

"I'll do it. I'm very distracting," May offered. She couldn't believe the words as they flew out of her mouth, but she ran with them anyway. She turned to Libby and tried to keep her smile in place as she said, "Why should the princess have all the adventures? It's my turn to be the hero. I'll go out the front door and make some noise. You guys go back out through the bathroom, then we'll all meet up at the entrance to the neighborhood, behind the big stone sign."

Trick said, "Cool, that's a cool idea. But I'll go with you. All three of us trying to get out that little window at once — no way. And two people can cause twice the distraction, right? Let me help."

May looked to Trick and asked, "Are you sure?"

"Positive," he said. He gave her a friendly smack on the arm and climbed the stairs, pausing on the small landing at the top.

May drew up right behind him, and Libby came behind her, with Jackdaw bringing up the rear. Trick plastered his right ear against the wood. "I think he's still upstairs," he told them, but he didn't sound that confident.

Libby reached past Trick and got a good grip on the knob. "On the count of three," she said. "Stay low, stay quiet. May, you and Trick run like hell." They nodded.

"One . . . two . . . *three!*"

She pressed the door open, controlled but fast.

It wasn't far for them to run. Just through the dining room and living room, then the front door — it was still hanging open, thank God.

May and Trick ducked outside and closed the door softly behind themselves, without even a telltale click.

Out onto the porch they toppled, down the porch steps and onto the lawn, where they stood still, and quiet, and watched the windows. Upstairs in what must have been one of the bedrooms, they saw the shape of a man glide past a curtain.

May shuddered. Trick did too. He looked to her and asked, "Now what?"

"Um . . ." She scanned the yard and didn't see much that looked useful for a distraction. A few shrubs, a concrete walkway, a weedy flower bed with a brick border. That gave her an idea. "You called in a break-in, right?"

"Yeah." He checked his watch. "Almost seven minutes ago. Maybe they thought it was a crank call."

"Or maybe they're just slow, and they need a little motivation." She went to the flower bed and wiggled a brick until it came loose from the soil.

"What are you . . . ? Oh."

"Stand back." She wound her arm back and hurled the brick at the living room window. The glass shattered; the brick snagged on the curtain and landed inside with a thud.

"Hey, Ken!" May shouted. Her own voice shocked her with its volume in the dull quiet of the suburban neighborhood. She wanted to cry, and she wanted to turn and run — but she couldn't do that, not until she'd stolen enough seconds from the Needle Man. Not until Libby had her head start. So she screamed this time, as loud as she could: "*I am Princess X!*"

Because she *was*, kind of. It had been half hers at the start: the princess with a sword, not a wand. And she was the one who'd embarked on the real-life quest and found the gray child, and she was the one trying to restore the princess's kingdom.

But May wasn't carrying a sword — just a multitool.

And the Needle Man was coming.

Kenneth Mullins stomped down the stairs and through the living room. He was shouting now too, one word over and over, and it sounded like "Christine."

"Trick!" May said, as loudly as she dared — her hand outstretched, fingers wiggling toward him.

He grabbed her hand. "You okay?"

"Yes!" she replied frantically.

The front door opened with a crash, and Ken stood on the threshold. She could see him over her shoulder, lit mostly from behind; he was a lanky man, tall and angular.

Holding a gun.

His eyes swept the lawn. May squeaked and Trick gasped as he spotted them. He raised the gun in their direction, and it all went so slowly — the moment stretched out like taffy.

Away. She had to lure him *away*.

She yanked Trick by the wrist, not toward the side of the house and the bathroom window there, but in the other direction — toward the empty lot next door, the one covered with trees that might hide them, or at the very least might lead Ken away from Libby.

The first gunshot was the loudest thing she'd ever heard. The second-loudest thing happened almost simultaneously, just a moment behind the bullet, when the pine trunk behind her shattered into a thousand pieces. She felt splinters firing past her, sticking in her hair and scratching at the side of her neck.

He'd seen them. He was coming for them. And that was good, because it meant he wasn't chasing Libby! Wasn't it? Now she wasn't so sure.

Trick grabbed her by the arm and pulled her hard, drawing her along in a zigzag pattern as another shot went off, and then a third. May didn't know where the other two bullets landed. She could barely hear anything anymore — only the long-running reverberation of the bullets, humming in the back of her head.

The trees were thicker than she'd realized when they'd started running toward them. She banged her shoulders, elbows, and knees on nubby stumps and the trunks of tall evergreens. Finally, when she felt they were far enough away to hide, she dropped to the ground. Trick fell down beside her.

They were no more than fifty yards from the house, but it felt like miles. They could see it, yes. But they couldn't see any sign of Libby or Jackdaw, and that was probably good.

Except that Ken heard something, back inside the house.

He turned and went back in, still carrying his gun. He didn't even shut the front door.

May's phone vibrated against her butt. Trick's phone was already in his hand. "It's Jack," he said. "He must have gotten out. He says to head for the road, he'll pick us up."

"In *what*?"

"It doesn't say — just *come on!*"

Then a scream rang out from inside the house, followed by another gunshot.

"Libby's still in there!" May shrieked.

And her hearing was coming back, for she heard her best friend's voice as clear as day from inside the living room. *"You leave them alone!"*

Sirens sounded in the distance, but it was difficult to feel much relief about them. Trick had a good grip on her arm. "The cops are coming! Stay here where it's safe!"

"No!" May climbed to her feet and staggered a few steps back toward the house. "You go! Keep going, find Jackdaw. I can't leave her. Not this time."

It was too late. She was back on the front lawn, the front door hanging open before her. Her own blood pumped in her ears, and her feet were banging against the wood plank porch and then the floor of the foyer. In the distance, the sirens were less and less far away. She prayed they were coming in fast.

May shouted, "Libby!"

She held her breath, only for a second — long enough to hear that she and Ken were farther back, beside the door to the basement. One of the rooms Jackdaw had opened, maybe.

"Libby! I'm coming!" she shouted.

And from that back room: "May, get out of here!"

But May didn't. Light was coming from a room at the end of the corridor. The Needle Man's shadow stretched out into the hall, his arms and legs as long and thin as hypodermics, and he was holding that gun in his hand. It was pointed at Libby, who crouched on the floor of the bedroom, eyes closed and breathing hard.

May froze against the wall, and something bulky pressed up against her thigh. She patted her pocket with her hand. Trick's multitool. She pulled it from her pocket and flipped the biggest blade out, and she stalked slowly toward the Needle Man.

Her feet were quiet, but the boards beneath them were squeaky, and she could hear herself breathing, the air captured in her lungs and lost, over and over and over. Too loud, too fast. It would never work. She was a bad liar and a worse ninja. But all she had to do was distract him, enough for the princess to escape.

"May, get out of here!" Libby screeched.

It was too late. She was right behind him. If he glanced over his shoulder, he'd see her.

He glanced. He saw her.

She slammed into him from the side — he'd turned, in that glancing second — and caught him at the elbow. He pushed her away, shoving her into the hall. But May wasn't hurt, she was only scared and angry — so when he retreated to regroup, she plowed forward again with the multitool. This time she knocked him backward, even farther into the room. He almost landed on top of Libby, who was up against the wall.

Libby lashed out with her feet. She swung her big black combat boots like a mace and connected with Ken's hip, his ribs, his arm. He did not drop the gun, but he fell to one knee, pivoted, and brought the gun back around — to point at May, whose heart almost stopped without the help of a bullet. Then he pointed back at Libby as he retreated, backing up toward the room's only window.

"You!" he said to May, though he kept the gun mostly aimed at Libby.

He might've said more, but something moved in the window behind him. A cinder block spun wildly through the glass, smacking Ken between the shoulder blades and clattering to the floor. The force of the blow toppled him toward May, and the gun aimed everywhere as he tried to get his balance back — the ceiling, the walls, the girls, the window behind him. He caught himself and pivoted again, spinning and sliding on the glass shards as May charged him, the multitool brandished before her.

Not a sword. Barely better than a penknife. But the blade jabbed hard into Ken's forearm.

He cried out and finally dropped the pistol, but the whole world was covered in broken glass, and for some reason, her hands were bleeding. Ken threw her off like a winter coat, and she cracked against the door frame face-first — she actually *heard* the crack, and was it her skull or the wood? She didn't know, but it was the third loudest thing she'd ever heard, and she dropped the multitool as she saw stars for the first time in her life. Real stars, not like cartoons. More like the sizzling sparkle of fading fireworks, trickling back down to earth, all light and ashes.

The gun went off. Who was holding it now? Ken had dropped it, hadn't he? Maybe no one was holding it, and it'd simply gone off in the fray. She couldn't see. There was shouting outside, and the red and blue lights added to the silver twinkle of the stars behind May's eyes.

She swayed on her feet, looking for the multitool. Ken was staggering almost as badly as she was, and Libby was scooting backward, then sideways — crablike — trying to dart past Ken and reach May.

But she saw the cinder block too, and so long as the Needle Man was standing, she wasn't finished with him. The block was heavy in her hands, so heavy she wasn't sure she could lift it — except that she was already holding it up, already rocking back and forth, working it up into an arc so that when she spun around and swung it . . . she hit him in the ribs, and he went down gasping.

The block slipped out of May's hands, scraping them raw as she let it fly. She slumped to her knees. But Libby was there. Libby had her.

"Up!" Libby gasped, and she clutched May around the chest, hauling her toward the hall. She half pushed, half dragged May forward while May worked to straighten her legs and make them work right again.

But she still was having trouble seeing straight, and for a ludicrous moment she laughed with relief that she no longer wore glasses. It was hard enough seeing double in contacts, and fortune-tellers were useless when they couldn't even see their shoes. But she could see hers. She could line them up, one in front of the other. She needed help, but she had help. She had Libby's arm holding her up, and then Trick was there too.

"Come on, we've got to get out of here!" he said, as he added his own arm to her support system.

May sagged, but Trick and Libby held her upright. They hustled out the front door, all three knocking against one another in the narrow opening, but then they were free — they were out of the house and down the porch, and into the yard again where she'd first declared that she was Princess X, and she wondered if it'd meant anything to Ken. She wondered if he'd heard her, or if he'd understood a word of it. There was no more noise back inside the house, no more gunshots and no more yelling.

She felt herself fading, but she was almost ready to quit fighting it, because it would be okay now, wouldn't it? Libby was alive, and Trick was there, and there were cop cars and the red and blue lights and sirens wailing a few blocks away, homing in.

There was a car, and Libby dragged May toward it. May didn't recognize the vehicle, but Jackdaw was driving it — and when the back door opened, she let her friends shove her inside it. Libby toppled in after her, and Trick went around to the passenger-side door. Once everyone was secure, Jackdaw threw the car in gear and the tires squealed as they peeled out of the driveway.

May's head was throbbing and she heard sirens, and she would probably hear sirens forever and ever, and there were worse things, so long as you knew they were coming to help. She put her head down on Libby's lap, and stared up at her eyes — which gazed back down at her with a worried expression.

"Hang in there, May. There's some blood, but it's not that bad. You're going to be fine."

She grinned. "I'm already fine. *Everything* is."

But she was very tired. *Miles* beyond tired, really. So since everything was fine, and Libby was alive, and the police were coming for the Needle Man . . . she closed her eyes and gave in, collapsing off to sleep.

TWENTY-FIVE

The girls sat on a curb outside the apartment building, fiddling with fat chunks of chalk. May drew her knees up to her chest, where she hugged them tightly, while Libby half reclined so she could reach farther and draw bigger. She used the side of her hand to blend the red and yellow together, creating more refined shadows in Princess X's dress. It was still pink, and still theatrical — but this version of the princess was older and taller. Her dress had a lower neckline and a more sophisticated cut. She looked like she was going to the Oscars instead of the prom.

She still looked like Libby, though.

May watched the self-portrait come together, filling the whole street corner almost. She didn't contribute to the artwork, because this version of Princess X wasn't hers. This was Libby's story, and May couldn't draw for crap anyway.

Her black eye was darker, more established now, the third day after Ken Mullins had been captured by the police. It was a fractured eye socket, the doctor said. It'd look worse before it looked better, but it'd be okay in the end — or so she was forced to believe, because it was either that or wander around with a lopsided face for the rest of her life.

"I forgot to tell you," Libby said, never taking her gaze away from the blossoming artwork. "They let Jackdaw go last night. They only held him a few days, because of you. You went to bat for him — and he didn't hurt anybody, and that lady got her car back. He didn't even scratch it."

"I don't remember much about it." She'd awakened on a gurney, in a room so bright she could hardly see anything. She remembered answering question after question, and she remembered saying something about Jackdaw, yes. *He's my friend, yes. He helped save us, yes. Don't you touch him.*

"You told them plenty about Ken too, and they charged him this morning. Kidnapping, murder, false imprisonment . . . I don't know why kidnapping and false imprisonment are different, but whatever. They've got him on a whole bunch of stuff. I'll probably have to testify when he goes to trial."

"Yeah, I guess you will."

"It's going to suck." Libby fell silent.

"What did I tell them about you?" May prompted her, trying to get some hint of her smile back. She remembered trying to explain — something about a princess, something about her best friend in the world, and needles, and dead mothers. She had tried to tell them everything, but the lights were so bright and her head was a little bit broken. She gave them the highlights reel in snippets and sound bites, and they probably thought it was all because of the concussion.

Libby said, "I don't know. But they didn't arrest me, so there's something."

"They wouldn't do that."

"Why not?" she asked, looking up at last. "I broke into a guy's house. I thought it'd take longer, I guess . . . that I'd probably spend a few nights in jail before I could prove who I am. Or before you could come around all the way, and stick up for me. Your dad helped, though. He remembered me."

"Of course he did. You were gone for three years, not three thousand."

"Do you think he minds my staying here? It's only a few days. . . ."

May grinned. "If he minded, I'd never let him hear the end of it. But it turns out, he's pretty cool. Much cooler than I thought. He said you're welcome to stay as long as you want. And that's why I'm starting to believe him, when he says he wants me to be happy."

"Of course he wants you to be happy! He's your *dad*."

"Yeah, but now he's really working for it, you know? Heck, he's even trying to help Trick because he's my friend, and Dad barely knows him."

"Help him *how*?"

"Since Trick helped solve a kidnapping and everything" — she gave Libby a sidelong smile — "UW is letting him appeal that whole scholarship thing. He might get it back, but he needs character references. Dad volunteered."

"Speaking of Trick, we should probably invite him out for hot chocolate this afternoon so he doesn't feel too left out."

May shrugged. "I'll text him and see if he's interested. He's a decent friend, and he's pretty good backup if you're storming an island."

"And he's not stupid," Libby granted. "That's worth something."

"I never would've found you without him."

Libby put the finishing touches on the princess's sword, leaning down to blow away the excess chalk. It was a good drawing — more like a mural than a sidewalk doodle. The weather wouldn't hold, so it wouldn't last the afternoon. But that was all right, May thought. There was plenty of time to draw another one.

Libby sat up and dusted her hands off on the top of her jeans. "May?"

"Yeah?"

"Everything's going to be okay again, isn't it?"

May nodded firmly. She said, "Of course it will. It already *is*."

"Only *kind* of," Libby said, and a flicker of worry flashed across her eyes. "I mean, I've always wanted to go to Japan . . . but now that I get to go . . . it's like . . . I don't speak Japanese or anything. And what if my grandmother doesn't like me?"

"She's going to love you. You're both practically ninjas."

"That's racist," Libby said, and chucked a piece of chalk at May's chest.

May chucked it right back. "It was *your* story."

"I know, I know. I'm kidding. Not about the Japan thing, though."

"But it's only a couple of months, right?"

Libby picked up another piece of chalk and twiddled it between her fingers. "That's the plan, but I don't have any other family, really. Mom and Dad are gone. Mom had a sister, but I never met her. She'll be at

Grandma's, though — we'll see if she's cool or not. I don't know how it's going to go. I don't know how we'll talk to each other, or if we'll like each other. . . ."

"It's going to be great," May declared. Frankly, as far as she was concerned, every day that Libby was alive was going to be great, for the rest of forever. "You'll get to know your mom's family, and you're always welcome to stay with me, wherever I'm at. Dad's already said it's fine, and if Mom makes a stink, I'll come live with Dad. See? You have options. You can do whatever you want."

"But that's the thing: I don't *know* what I want. I spent so much time wanting to get away, and then I got away. Then I spent so much time wanting to find you and get my life back. Then I found you, and I got my life back."

"Technically, *I'm* the one who found *you*."

"Oh, shut *up*." Libby smiled hugely. "You know what I mean. I mean . . . now what?"

May considered this. She picked up a yellow nub of chalk and drew a little spiral on the sidewalk. "Now . . . now everything else happens . . . the whole rest of your life. You'll catch up in school, and then you'll apply to college. Probably, you'll want to go to UW, because that's where I'm going — and you'll want a roommate who you know for sure won't drive you crazy."

Libby's smile almost wobbled, but didn't quite. "You were always a good storyteller."

"And a great fortune-teller, remember? But I'm a *terrible* liar," she said earnestly. "So you might as well go along with it."

"Then keep talking, I'm listening. . . ."

"Right. So then what happens is, we both get jobs doing . . . whatever, you know. If we don't earn enough money to live off campus, we could probably just stay here with my dad. He's gone all the time anyway. I'll major in English or something, and you'll major in art. We'll start writing *Princess X* together again, maybe put some advertising on the website, maybe line up some official merch to sell." May frowned suddenly. "People are making a butt load of money off Princess X, and that should be *us* instead. Or you, anyway. It's your stuff they're ripping off."

"Most of it's just fan art," Libby argued gently. "Nobody really makes a butt load. Almost all of them do it for fun."

"For fun is okay. Selling stickers and patches and stuff . . . that's not okay."

"Maybe you should go to law school. You could be my lawyer."

May put on a thoughtful face and nodded. "That would be neat. I could write *epic* takedown notices. Together, we could rule the Internet."

"You can be my avenging knight. Ooh!" Libby said, grabbing the yellow nub away from May. "That's what Princess X needs next: an avenging knight."

"You think?"

"I've already decided. Your armor is gold, and you're carrying a black battle-ax."

"A black battle-ax? Why?"

"Because everybody knows that black is the coolest color. What color do you want your hair to be?"

"Well, *now* I want it to be black," May said.

"I say we make you a redhead. You've got a little red in your hair, someplace. When the sunlight hits it just right."

"We're in Seattle. How often does the sunlight hit anything?"

"Walgreens is right down the street. We could get a box of dye. It'd surprise the heck out of your dad."

"You're going to make me do this, aren't you?"

Libby shook her head, but she didn't shake the smile. "No, May. I'm not going to make you do anything, except help me finish the story."

THE END

ACKNOWLEDGMENTS

This has been my first foray into young adult literature, and it's been an amazing experience all around. I couldn't have done it without a whole team of wonderful folks, not least of all my long-suffering husband, Aric Annear; my agent, Jennifer Jackson; my editor, Cheryl Klein — and the marvelous production team at Scholastic. Many undying thanks to the lot of them, for their support, encouragement, and whip-cracking as necessary.

This book was edited by Cheryl Klein and designed by Phil Falco. The production was supervised by Elizabeth Starr Baer and Elizabeth Krych. The text was set in Alisal, with display type set in Bureau Eagle. This book was printed and bound by R.R. Donnelley in Crawfordsville, Indiana. The manufacturing was supervised by Shannon Rice.